ANN MCNICOL

Cyanea

Charlies Story Volume 4

"In the long history of humankind (and animal kind, too), those who learned to collaborate and improvise most effectively have prevailed."

Charles Darwin

Contents

Chapter 1 ~Prologue ~Blue Octopus

Heron Island, Great Barrier Reef Australia, 2046

The blue octopus nestled in the finger coral, his tentacles wrapped around the base as he watched divers move along the reef slope. His colors matched the surroundings so well that he was invisible. It was early morning, and the reef was coming to life. Purple sea fans swayed with the pulsing water, and schools of fish moved around and through coral canyons. The octopus wasn't concerned; divers were frequent visitors on the reef and seemed harmless.

One diver paused, looking at the finger coral. Something had caught her attention, but it took a while for her to see him. It was the octopus's large expressive eyes and pulsating head ridges that caused her to draw a deep breath and hold her position. Today, her team was checking the slope for coral bleaching and assessing coral health, a constant concern in warmer seas. However, Alana had a special interest in octopuses, her primary field of research back in the United States. She signaled her team to pause, moved to a patch of sand, and settled in to watch the creature.

The octopus looked at Alana and wondered if he had seen this diver before. He thought so. Some divers brought treats, and this could be one. Releasing his hold on the coral, he jetted into the water and floated down, spreading his arms like a net, and settled onto the sand. He was still a safe distance but near enough for Alana to see him clearly. She reached into her bag to retrieve a small crab for her visitor.

He released his hold on the coral and rose into the open water. Using a pulsing motion, he moved close to Alana, then settled onto the sand before her. He reached for the crab with a tentacle. After eating, he moved toward Alana, walking across the sand on his tentacles.

He gazed into her mask for one still moment, making eye contact. Then he reached and embraced her with all eight arms, gave a squeeze, then released and jetted away.

Alana looked at the space where the blue octopus had been, now a wispy cloud of black ink. She shook her head, and a burst of bubbles came from her regulator. With her subject gone, she packed up her camera, swam over to her dive partner, signaling her excitement with her hands, and motioned for him to follow her back to their boat.

Dave gave her a thumbs-up and wrote "Wow" on his slate. Then he added, "That was wild."

"Yes, it was," Alana replied, pointing toward the boat. They were on the reef slope at a depth of fifteen meters and had been underwater for almost forty-five minutes. It was time to surface.

At that depth, all colors other than blue were gone. The reef was majestic. A grouper eyed Alana from beneath a ledge while large schools of surgeonfish and snappers darted between coral heads and filled the reef with motion.

Reaching the boat, Alana handed the camera gear to Jim, the team member charged with monitoring the two of them while they were below.

He took the equipment and helped her into the boat. "Anything unusual?"

Alana tossed her gear under the bench. "Yes, wait until you see the video. I just got a hug from an octopus!"

Her dive partner, Dave, climbed onboard. "I got it on camera, too. That was amazing."

Jim looked at the sky, with dark clouds marching toward them.

"It's good you guys came back a bit early. I've been watching the sky, and I think we are in for some nasty weather. Unless you guys really need to go back down, we should skip a second dive and head in." Jim didn't mention the shark he had been watching. Alana, like many Americans, seemed skittish around sharks.

Alana nodded. "I agree. As much as I'd like another dive, this is my last day on the island, and I wouldn't like it to end with an uncomfortable trip back in a thunderstorm."

"When do you head back to the States?" Jim asked.

"I leave for Brisbane tomorrow and have three days to finish my lab work, write my final reports, and pack up. I leave for the States on Friday."

As she dried her hair with a towel, a fin appeared just off the back of the boat. They all watched as a sizable tiger shark swam by.

"Just our luck," Dave said.

"What luck?" Alana asked.

"If he'd come earlier, we could've gotten some great shots."

Alana laughed. "I can live without taking pictures of a tiger shark. I'd rather watch from up here."

She looked thoughtful and added, "I hope our octopus friend is okay."

"Me too, Dave said.

Chapter 2 ~Samantha~ Home

Coastal Eleven, Georgia Barrier Island, December 2046

Not many days felt perfect, but today was one of them. We sat on a marina bench, waiting to board the ferry to Coastal Eleven. The sun warmed my shoulders, and Peter's hand in mine left me feeling flushed and warm. He squeezed my hand and pointed to a brown pelican as it swooped down and landed in front of us on the water.

"Samantha, I love seeing you so happy. I wish we could get to Coastal Eleven more often," Peter said.

"So do I, but it's called paying our dues. But yes, I'm happy we will have Christmas on the island. I miss Mom and Jerry. I miss Charlie. The island still feels like home."

I watched to see how Peter reacted. We had our own place in married student housing at Georgia State. The small one-bedroom Atlanta flat was our home now. I love our place, but sometimes, I wake up trying to hear the seabirds and waves. Part of me will always think of Coastal Eleven as home.

Peter seemed fine and gave my hand a squeeze as if to say he understood.

He lifted my hand and gave it a kiss. "I didn't grow up on the island, but it feels like home, too. I'm glad I lived there for your 'gap year.' Our apartment in Atlanta can't compare to an island surrounded by a coral reef."

He pulled me in for a hug. We'd been married almost two years, but sometimes, I still felt like a newlywed and kept looking to see who was watching.

The island was my home for a long, long time. Dad had been a research biologist stationed on the barrier islands. He monitored the effects of flooding and worked with bioengineered corals. The project developed corals that would grow in warmer waters and succeeded more than anyone expected. His team's work was why we have coral reefs all along the Georgia and Florida coastlines.

When I was ten, Dad started taking me with him on his reef walks. Mom was also a scientist, but she studied tides and currents. Dad was all about corals and the animals that lived on the reef. By the time I was twelve, I was spending part of my day working with Dad and learning a ton of marine biology. He died that year. The institute kept us at Coastal Eleven so Mom could continue her work, and I started going out on my own. Like Dad, I kept detailed observational journals and shared them with his boss at the institute.

Our island was far enough from the mainland that my brother Jerry and I couldn't go to a *normal* school. I was enough of a science geek and loner that online school suited me. Then, one day, while on a reef walk, an octopus approached me. That was Charlie, and that was how we discovered the local super-intelligent octopus population we call the *Nest*. The ones who could communicate. I was not going to say they talk. It took a computer translation program for us to understand each other. Since then, we'd discovered sentient octopuses in Cuba.

When I was working with the research institute studying the octopuses, I met Peter. He was sixteen, tall, cute, and smart. I had an insane crush from day one.

I looked up just as the ferry approached.

"Time to go," Peter said as he stood, stretched, and pulled our bags from underneath the bench.

The catamaran pulled silently into the harbor. I heard that in the old days when boats used combustion engines. They were noisy and gave off clouds of smoke. I'd only known electric engines, and these could have been sailboats. They were silent. The pelican finally noticed the vessel and moved out of the way. We caught up with the crowd as they crossed the walkway and stepped out onto the deck.

I felt the difference immediately. We were in the harbor, and there was no wave action, but standing on the deck felt different from standing on land. There was a gentle, almost imperceptible movement beneath our feet. I'd traveled this ferry hundreds of times and loved the feeling of being out on the ocean. *Could life get any better?*

"It's good to see a smile on your face," Peter said.

"You know me. Being on the water is the best."

"I love it too. I'm glad Cuba didn't spoil that for us."

Cuba. I felt the smile leave my face. We had a seriously crazy time of it when a fringe group of activists abducted us from a research station. I shook it off. Today was a good day. I wouldn't let dark memories ruin it. We were going home. It would be great to see Mom, my little brother Jerry, and Charlie. Oh, and Mark, too. He counted as honorary family now that he and Mom were officially a couple living together. I couldn't really call Jerry my little brother anymore now that he was taller than I was.

As our ferry pulled out of the harbor, Peter and I settled into chairs on the open deck, ignoring the indoor air-conditioned *lounge*. We both preferred to experience fresh air and watch for dolphins, turtles, and other creatures as they surfaced. Once, I even saw a huge manta ray that must have been five meters across.

I couldn't help thinking about being held prisoner in Cuba for almost three months. They kept us locked up in cabins, and sometimes, I felt like the walls were closing in on me. I was not angry at the Cubans or

Cuba. We met lots of great people at the research station, and when we were rescued, the Cuban officials were wonderfully caring. There were "bad" people in every country, and really, not all our kidnappers were Cubans.

Why would anyone kidnap a seventeen-year-old? Well, Peter was nineteen, but I think they kidnapped Peter because he was with me. They were after me. I was the one who discovered a race of super-intelligent octopuses living on the reef off Coastal Eleven. For a long time, I was the primary contact for their interactions with humans.

When the scientists released genetically modified corals to expand the reef systems, they never expected an evolutionary hotspot. They never expected we would end up with talking, intelligent octopuses. But there you have it.

The kidnappers wanted me to establish contact and communication with the Cuban octopuses. Crazy. We were unable to contact anyone, and I was terrified. I was seventeen, and the experience was traumatic on multiple levels.

Throughout the whole ordeal, Peter was there for me. He was strong and steady and kept me grounded. I don't know that I could have held it together if he hadn't been with me. It was while they held us captive that my feelings crystallized.

Shortly after the officials stormed the island where they had us captive, Peter asked if I would marry him, and I said *yes*.

We planned for a long engagement, waiting until we graduated with our bachelor's degrees. Not that I really cared, but Mom went ballistic about me getting married at seventeen. I point out that I would be nineteen when we married, and Peter would be twenty-one. We were young, but both of us were intelligent, mature, and knew what we wanted.

Peter was the perfect gentleman and kept our courtship what he called "age-appropriate." He moved into the guest room in Mark's cottage, continuing his studies online and working with the octopus project all through my self-imposed gap year. When Peter returned to campus to complete his degree, he stayed with his folks in Atlanta. Mom relented and let me visit and stay with them.

Peter studied for two majors: biology and public relations. He's currently working on a Doctorate in Public Policy in Science. So, we are one big NOAA family. Dad, or I should say, Dr. Martel Billings, my father, would have been proud. And it made sense that we all continued his work. I wondered what he would think of our partnership with smart, communicating octopuses?

We were the only ones getting off at Coastal Eleven, and by the time we reached our island, the ferry was almost empty. I was both hungry and impatient to get there. I hadn't been home in months, and I was aware we would only be on the island for a bit over a week. Peter had meetings set up in the new year, and I had a full schedule of seminars.

As we pulled into the harbor, Mom waved to us. We had a welcoming committee.

"I think they're glad to see us," Peter said.

"Is that Alana?" I asked.

Peter strained to look. "I think it is. Were you expecting her to be at Coastal Eleven?"

"I didn't even know she was back from Australia."

"Welcome home," Mom said, wrapping me in a bear hug.

When I came up for air and stepped back, Jerry rushed to Peter. I was only a bit jealous. Jerry adored Peter. He was the older brother Jerry wished for. Peter filled a hole in his life, too.

Mark was right behind Jerry, smiling ear-to-ear. I was glad things were working out between him and Mom. I liked to think of Mom having a family again.

Mark said, "Jerry and I will take your bags to the cottage. Why don't you go up with Amanda and Alana? We have some snacks ready, and

Amanda will put tea on. We'll join you in a bit."

"Thanks, tea sounds great."

Chapter 3~ Charlie ~ New Responsibility

Coastal Eleven, Barrier Reef, Georgia, 2046

Small fish moved through sea fans in motions that seemed random. When I was a Youngling, my mentor made me watch the chaos until I saw the patterns and could successfully hunt. We all learned that the patterns weren't random at all. I grew up hunting and eating these fish.

Other brightly colored fish swam in and out of sight as if to taunt me. These small, flashy fish moved less cautiously. They tasted bitter, and we never ate them. Archimedes thought it humorous that I tried eating colorful fish in Cuba. They looked different, and I was curious. But, like our brightly colored fish, they were not good to eat.

It was time Runt and I resumed more of our duties. There had been two Youngling broods raised since our return. Details of our adventure had faded, and I had difficulty retrieving some events. But then a question or a comment from Archimedes triggered a memory, and my ridges pulsed so rapidly that others moved away in alarm. The worst was when I would look for my old friend, Learner, forgetting that she stayed behind on the Cuban reef. It was good that Runt returned with me, and we could remind each other and confer on the events we experienced.

Learner and I traveled on the humans' boat to Cuba when Samantha and Peter went missing. The Nest sent us because of my connection with

Samantha, and Learner's communication skills with wild octopuses. We were spies, hoping to use information from the local populations to find them. We succeeded, much to everyone's relief.

Learner was brash and overconfident, but she did it. She broke through to the Cuban octopuses and got the information we needed. It turned out the Cuban octopuses were like us. They had Nests with social structures like ours! Their language was different enough to be a challenge, and Learner stayed in Cuba to continue working on learning their messaging. She wanted to become fluent.

No one from the Nest had ever traveled as far as we did, and no one had met Brothers who spoke a different language. Our world had changed almost as much as when we discovered that humans could communicate with us.

With Samantha safe, my tension eased, and the journey home seemed to take forever. Runt and I spent the time in a glass container with a few barren rocks scattered on the bottom. The humans brought food for us regularly. We were comfortable but bored. Samantha sat outside the container and visited. When she went to rest, Jerry or Peter stayed with us. After endless light and dark periods, they carried us in the transport container to our reef slope. We were home. The full Elder Council and many Brothers assembled to welcome us.

Once the crowd dispersed, I remember feeling joy and belonging at being on my home reef. It was a shock to realize that the sounds and sights of each reef are unique. Cuba was similar but different. The clicking of parrotfish grazing on rocks covered with algae, the sounds of waves crashing on the crest, and even the taste of the water felt like home. *This was my reef, with the fish from my home.*

Some things had changed. I was no longer active with the wild octopus project. But the project continued. While Learner was not here, many of her Brothers took over the project. Her brood were all raised from wild octopus eggs, and they had a vested interest in the project. The Elder Council encouraged me to hand off my responsibility for the work. At first, I struggled with anger. I had started the project. Archimedes helped me see the logic and need for me to let others continue to advance our understanding.

He was firm with me with me. *"It is time to let the next generation take over the project. They have been working in your absence and are making good progress. The Council has other work for you."*

"What work?" I asked.

Archimedes' colors shifted to the blues and greens, showing his amusement at my question. *"They want you working with the humans."*

"I do that. I need more work. We do not meet very often."

"The Elders Council wants you to ask for more meetings. They want you to ask for meetings so that you and Runt can learn about the rules that humans follow."

"Why?"

"We need to understand humans. We need to know how they make and enforce their rules."

What he suggested would be an enormous and vital task. The suggestion came close to overwhelming me. Archimedes and the Council were correct. We knew little about the human way of life and how they made their rules, and it had become clear that humans had an enormous impact on the ocean and our lives.

"We should know more about humans," I agreed. *"I can ask for meetings dedicated to teaching human ways. Will you attend the meetings?"*

"I will attend when I can. But the Elder Council wants you and Runt to make learning about humans your primary responsibility. They want you in the Council meetings to keep us informed of human actions and rules that might put us in danger and impact our lives. In time, they hope we of the Nest can be an active voice in how humans make their rules."

"I will ask for a meeting and request lessons on human culture. Let us see how they respond."

Archimedes signaled approval and left.

Chapter 4 ~Samantha~ Christmas Visitor

It felt like we never left. Peter and I were back in our "honeymoon cottage," except now we had a guest in the spare room.

"Nice cottage," Alana said.

"It has a history," Peter said. "Dr. Kelly built it when he stationed Mark on the island. When Samantha came home for her gap year, Mark was kind enough to let me move into the guest room."

"Alana, it is great to see you," Peter said.

"I hope it's okay that Amanda offered to put me in your guest room."

"No problem. I love that you came!" I said.

Alana was one of our oldest friends, and we had seen little of her in the last few years. When I first met Alana, I was only fourteen, and she was working at NOAA as a biologist. It was her first job out of college. Despite our age differences, almost ten years, we ended up friends. Dr. Kelly introduced us because she was the resident octopus specialist, and I was trying to make sense of my rather strange interaction with Charlie.

Actually, we didn't hit off at first. She was keeping an octopus in an aquarium, and I thought that was cruel. Alana quickly became part of our octopus language project and embraced our current policy: octopuses were intelligent and had rights. We did not hold them captive.

Alana stopped collecting and holding octopuses once she observed my interactions with Charlie. The young octopus was using a type of sign language to attempt communication. It took the computer language geeks months to work out a translation program, but now, we communicated using a display mat to generate color sequences.

Alana had changed little. She was still a perky blond with a ready smile and penetrating eyes. She looked fit, and I guessed she'd been doing lots of fieldwork during the visiting professorship appointment at the University of Queensland in Australia. The appointment was a huge thing. International travel was difficult and expensive. The support was part of an international initiative to build a worldwide perspective on climate change among scientists. I was suitably jealous that she had been to the Great Barrier Reef.

Peter finished pouring a cup of tea for each of us.

"When did you get back from Australia?" he asked.

"Last month, and trying to get caught up has me almost manic. But Steve mentioned you were going to be at Coastal Eleven for Christmas. I called Amanda and wrangled an invitation."

Peter and I exchanged a look. "Well, we are honored you fit us in so soon. I want to hear all about Australia."

"Part of why I'm here is to talk about Australia. Heron Island and Reef are amazing. And they have octopuses. Really neat octopuses."

"Neater than Charlie?"

"Well, maybe not neater than Charlie. But they are still very cool. The species is *cyanea.* They're called the blue octopus. We'll talk about them soon. I need to apologize first."

"For what?" I asked.

"For not being supportive when you planned your wedding. I should have kept my thoughts to myself. I'm sorry."

"It's okay, Alana. You weren't alone in thinking we were rushing it. Nineteen was ridiculously young, and I wanted a small wedding. It was Mom and Dr. Kelly who sent a bunch of invitations out. I'm sorry we made you feel uncomfortable."

"Well, it's been two years, and you're doing great. Amanda said you're holding off on having kids for a while, and that's smart. I still don't understand why you wanted to get married so young, but you're doing okay."

Peter squeezed my hand. "It just sort of fell into place. We didn't want to wait."

"Alana, the kidnapping was awful, but it crystallized my feelings. I was done waiting to see if Peter was the man I wanted to spend my life with. He was the real deal, and I wanted it to be official."

"Ditto," Peter said.

"Samantha, how did you get your mom on board? You weren't even old enough to drink."

I laughed. "It was a battle. Peter stayed out of it as much as he could. I think it was a combination of being so glad I was home, alive and safe—and wanting to make me happy."

Peter added, "I think Samantha could have asked for anything, but Amanda drove a hard bargain. We had to wait until Sam turned nineteen, and both of us graduated with our bachelor's degrees to have her blessing."

"You forgot the provision that we had to behave ourselves," I added.

Alana rolled her eyes. "You're kidding."

"Well, Amanda didn't insist on chaperoned dates, but when Samantha stayed in Atlanta, she had her own room at my parents' house. When I stayed here at Coastal Eleven, I stayed in Mark's guest room. That's the one you're in now."

I laughed. "It was kind of funny, but it was also sweet. Kind of romantic."

"Okay, I'm glad Amanda had you wait. Not so much because of your age, but because you were fresh from a traumatic event. But you guys are doing fine. Again, I apologize."

Peter took my hand and pulled me in for a side hug. "Well, Samantha does everything on her own timeline. She was a NOAA intern at fourteen."

I said, "I wasn't an intern until I was sixteen. Before that, I was an unpaid volunteer."

"Your mom treated me to seeing your wedding album. It looks like it was a great party. I'm sorry I missed it."

Peter said, "It was. Dr. Snyder arranged passage for my parents and best friends from high school and college. Captain John brought them over on the university research vessel. They said they felt like royalty."

"The party was a beach cookout. Nothing fancy, but it was so much fun. And they set us up with a glamping tent on the other side of the island. Our private getaway for after the party."

"You camped for a honeymoon?"

"Yeah, it was silly but also nice. The tent had a queen-sized bed, a place to make coffee, and two seats to watch the sunrise. It was perfect."

Peter said, "And no one gave Samantha a hard time when I handed her an illegal glass of champagne to toast at our wedding."

We all had a good laugh.

"Where do you stay when you're at Coastal Eleven now?"

Peter said, "Here, in our very own cute cottage."

Alana shook her head. "I'm impressed that NOAA did that. A whole second habitat? I think you might have had some strings pulled on your behalf."

I shook my head and laughed. "They didn't build it for *us*. NOAA put the cottage on Coastal Eleven when they stationed Mark there."

Alana grinned. "How long did Mark last, staying in his own place?"

"I'm guessing he gradually moved in with Mom. By the time we got married, the unit was empty. We've had fun decorating it. I mean, it isn't really ours. It's guest accommodation for NOAA when we aren't there."

Peter got up and poured more tea for each of us and put a plate of cookies on the table. Alana and I each helped ourselves to one.

Peter said, "Okay, tell us about Australia. Tell us about this octopus."

"It's *octopus cyanea.* I only came across them on my last trip out to Heron Island, but the people I worked with have spent the last year studying their behavior. They live in colonies, and from what we've seen, it's that with the right people and the right tools, communication could be established. The team has been following your work here and in Cuba, and they think they have another sentient population."

"After our experience in Cuba, I shouldn't be surprised at the idea of intelligent octopuses in other locations," Peter said.

"Well, I am a bit," I said. "We figured the Cuban octopuses and Georgia octopuses are related. I'm not sure we can make the same argument about Australia."

Alana said, "We've always known octopuses are intelligent. Maybe we just never knew how to talk to them before."

I shook my head. "No, we know there are what the Nest calls 'wild octopuses' that don't communicate. These are solitary animals and never developed a social structure. The Nest can't communicate with them either."

Alana said, "Well, cyanea are living in colonies. They hunt cooperatively, and the researchers say that observations support the theory that *cyanea* use sophisticated communication between individuals."

My head was spinning as I tried to take this in. "I need an email for the lead researcher. Can you give me an introduction? Let them know I'll be in contact?"

Alana chuckled. "The lead researcher is Dr. Snyder, and he knows all about you and Peter, and the work on Coastal Eleven. Part of the reason I'm here is to pitch an invitation to both of you. They want you to apply for the visiting scientist program."

I sat in a silence of confusion. Australia? It was on the other side of the world. But, it was also the Great Barrier Reef.

When I didn't say anything, Alana continued her pitch, "Sam, they really want to get an octopus communication program started. Think about it."

Peter moved in beside me and whispered, "Are you recovered enough for another adventure? It's your call. "

"I don't know. We'll think about it."

I knew Peter wanted to go, but did I?

Chapter 5 ~ Charlie ~ Negotiations

I waited for Samantha at our lagoon meeting site. My ridges pulsed with nervous energy as I watched for a shadow on the sand to announce the arrival of a boat. Usually, I looked forward to seeing Samantha and the NOAA team, but this would be an uncomfortable meeting. No matter how I phrased the Elder's request, the humans would feel we were criticizing their society. How could they not?

That was what the Elders were doing. Samantha was a good person, and NOAA had put efforts into keeping poachers off our reef. But while they assured us it was "illegal" for poachers to come, they were vague in how they would prevent or punish the activity. And the Elders were asking tough questions. A growing concern throughout the Nest was that human activities might have caused white coral to appear in warmer times. They helped us treat the coral, but were they causing the disease? If our reef died, we died.

I agreed with the Elders. We needed to know more about humans and did not even know the questions to ask. They said they were our partners on the reef. It was time that we learned much more about who they were. This was our home; we should be part of the Council's decisions concerning human activities on or affecting the reef.

Today's meeting will be uncomfortable. I wonder who will be with today's team. I wish the Council had given today's task to another Elder, but I can see I was the obvious choice.

There was no way to warn NOAA about why we were requesting a meeting. The call button NOAA installed announces that we wish for a meeting on the next high tide. Today, my job would be to explain our concerns and ask that they share enough information so that we could be true partners—and be part of making rules for what humans did on the reef.

A large crab emerged from the rubble. Most likely, he was after the same fish I had been watching. The crab was tasty. Soon, a familiar shadow crossed the sand beneath us. I watched above as the boat attached to the secured buoy. Three humans entered the water and glided to the sand, joining Runt and me.

Samantha was easy to recognize. She was the only female human who came to our meetings. The other two were male. It was likely that Peter was the human next to Samantha. I moved closer and confirmed Jerry was working the camera. I could recognize him because his head was light, and Peter and Samantha were dark. Humans did not change color.

As soon as I recognized Samantha and Jerry, I saw my colors lighten and the pulsing of my ridges ease. I trusted them both and knew Jerry almost as well as Samantha, my first human friend.

Samantha rolled the communication mat onto the sand, connected her tablet, and typed. Soon, a sequence of colors flashed across the mat and conveyed her message.

"It is good to see you, Charlie. Dr. Snyder said the Nest requested a meeting. Is there a problem? Have you found white coral again?"

"There is no urgent problem. The Brothers treat the white coral when it arrives using your probiotic. It is a different problem, and I am unsure how to express it. We might not have the right words yet."

"I understand. Try to explain, and when words are an issue, we will work on finding the right word. It has been a while since we added to our shared dictionary."

"Your team visits the Nest. You see how we live, teach our Younglings, and how the Elder Council decides. But we cannot visit your Nests or observe how you teach Younglings. We do not know how your Council decides, and your decisions and actions affect us here on the reef."

I paused and noted that Jerry was working the camera and that the other human had moved close to Samantha. As he came close, I recognized that this was the human called Peter. I could hear the vibrations as they communicated with each other.

"Charlie, what you say is true, but it would be too dangerous for you or your kind to visit on land. What does your Council want us to do?

"They want you to teach Runt and me about human Nests so we can share this knowledge."

"I don't understand. I've always answered questions the best that I could. What does the Council want to know?" Samantha asked.

"We don't know the questions to ask. It's obvious that our reef, our world, is affected by human actions. We are glad of your efforts to keep humans from preying on octopuses. But we suspect human actions affect the reef that we are only beginning to see, like the white coral that can destroy our hunting grounds."

Samantha turned to Peter, and again, I could feel the vibrations in the water. How strange that they communicated with sound. When they finished, Peter moved to the tablet and typed.

"Humans also study the customs and way of life of distant humans. They are called Anthropologists, and they study how other humans gather food, mate, raise young, and organize for defense. Is this what they are asking you to do?"

"Yes, the Elders want to strengthen the ties between the Nest and humans. We want to have a say in human decisions that affect our home. We can only do this if we know more about you."

Again, Peter composed the message.

"We need to talk to NOAA and other 'Elders' of ours, but I believe we can do what you ask."

"Will you be our mentor?" I asked Peter.

"I need to consult with NOAA to work out a means for doing what you ask. We need to prepare lessons and develop new tools to communicate complicated information. We need to ask our Elders to assign a team dedicated to this task."

"I understand. The Elder Council does not make this request lightly. They know it will not be easy to learn your ways. But if we are to work together to protect the reef, we must understand more about each other. You have been learning about the Nest. We need to learn about humans."

Once again, we waited while Peter and Samantha exchanged vibrations. Jerry came closer and made vibrations, too. They stopped, and Samantha came to the mat.

"You and Runt will share a responsibility that will take much of your time, and this will need to be a long-term project. Human society is varied and complicated. We can start by building our shared vocabulary. However, we must also develop new tools to communicate complicated information. We will discuss this with NOAA."

"Will you be part of this team from NOAA?"

Samantha messaged, "You will need someone stationed at Coastal Eleven so they can meet with you often. But we will be part of the project, and we will come as often as we can."

Peter moved forward and added to her message, "I will ask to be part of the team, so I can select information and plan a logical sequence for delivery."

My ridges pulsed, and my colors turned dark. *"I trust you will not be too selective. We know there are humans who do not follow the rules. Please do not gloss over important facts. We need a thorough understanding."*

Samantha responded, "It will be a balance. If we try to present all the information, you will die of old age before you learn it all."

"Then Younglings will take over the task, and our Elders will continue

learning the ways of humans. Samantha, I am glad you will join us when you can, and that Peter will prepare the materials. Will you help NOAA choose a suitable mentor to head the team?"

"You need someone who lives on the island so you can meet frequently. Mark might take on the role, but we can't speak for him. If he is not willing, NOAA will station another human on the island."

"Mark would be good. I hope he agrees to be our mentor. But I wish you and Peter still lived on the island."

Samantha messaged, "I miss you when I'm away, and often wish I still lived on the island. But in some ways, I am still a Youngling and still learning. Peter and I must go where we can learn and be ready to be Elders."

"Samantha, we are now using distant communication tools to communicate with Learner on the Cuban reef. Could you and Peter communicate with us the same way?"

Vibrations filled the water as all three humans *talked*.

Samantha worked the display mat, her message flashing before me. "Maybe, but not immediately. I will talk to the computer team about this."

"Why can't we use the same equipment we used to communicate with Learner?"

"They designed the system for octopus-octopus communication. That means both sites are underwater and require a human on each site to work equipment and mediate communication. I don't think it will be difficult to adjust the program with one site on land and the other on the reef. If anything, it should be easier. But I need to talk to the computer team."

I felt my colors lighten with this message. *Maybe I could meet with Samantha and Peter when they were away from Coastal Eleven.* This thought made me happy.

Chapter 6 ~Home Dynamics

Jerry finished putting the equipment away. With no compressor on the island, we needed to exchange tanks between dives. It was heavy work. If NOAA agrees to host an instructional mentor to meet with Charlie and Runt daily, they would need to expand the solar array and provide a compressor.

"Are you coming over for lunch?" Jerry asked.

"After we clean up and change," I said. "Well, Peter and I will be over, Alana said she has a report she needs to finish."

Jerry looked around the room. "I'm glad we have the cottage here and you have a place of your own. Fitting five in our house would feel cramped, fitting six would be a mess."

I laughed and rolled my eyes. "You're just happy to have your room to yourself!"

"Well, that too."

"We're happy to have the cottage. But you don't get rid of us that easy. Expect to see a lot of us in the main house. We are here to visit.

Jerry turned red. "I didn't mean it that way."

"I'm kidding, Brother. I know you miss me."

"I did miss you. I'm glad you guys made it for the holidays this year."

"We are, too," Peter said.

I pulled Jerry in for a hug. "I miss you a lot while I'm away."

"I'm glad you guys are coming up for lunch." he said. "We'll have time to catch up.".

"We're looking forward to hearing all the details. And, lunch will be nice. Mom's making her noodle surprise casserole."

"Cool, I'll see you in a bit, I'm sure you guys want to settle in. Mom and Mark will be wondering where I am."

He left, heading back to the main Coastal Eleven Habitat. Peter and I had our kitchen, but we enjoyed having meals together. Sometimes, Mom and Mark cooked, and sometimes, Peter and I cooked. So far, Jerry had been off the hook, but he was good about setting the table and cleaning up.

Todays lunch would be special. Mom's surprise casserole had mushrooms, sunflower seeds, yogurt, and cheese. It was creamy and delicious. She made it when Peter and I visited because she knew it was a favorite of mine.

"What do you think Dr. Kelly will do with Charlie's request?" Peter asked.

"He might need our cottage to house a new team member. It will be an almost full-time job if they do it right."

Peter nodded, looking around our home away from home. "You could be right unless Mark wants to take it on."

"We can discuss it at lunch and see if he's interested. He's out on the reef daily, but I don't know if teaching about human government will appeal to him at all."

Peter finished preparing the lemonade. His expression told me his thoughts were far away.

"What's up?" I asked.

"The timing is off, but I'm tempted to ask for the job. Teaching the Nest about the mechanics of human government would check a lot of boxes on what I'd like to be doing."

"Wow," I said. "Maybe we should talk about what we want to do for the next year or two. I was keen on applying for the visiting scientist positions at the University of Queensland."

Peter smiled. "Me too. That's why I say the timing is off. But it isn't a given that we would both get visiting scientist positions in Queensland. Working on this project could be our Plan B."

"Yes, but I'm not sure we should consider it Plan B. The visiting scientist position is temporary, and I'm not sure I want to be that far away from Charlie and the Nest for a year. And I sure wouldn't go unless you were going."

"It's good to have options. Let's get Mark and Dr. Kelly's thoughts on it."

"Yeah, but I'm good at predicting how things will shake out. I can't see Dr. Kelly and NOAA saying no to this. I don't think they can if they want to maintain a relationship with the Nest."

He nodded in agreement.

"And Peter, if we apply to the University of Queensland for guest scientist positions, they will accept us. Alana said as much."

Lunch was nice. It felt like a scene from an old TV show, with Mom, Dad, and the kids sitting around a table. Peter and I weren't kids anymore. We were married adults visiting. Even Jerry was almost grownup. Anyway, it felt good.

The table went uncharacteristically quiet when Peter presented Charlie's request and what it would entail. Mom broke the silence first. She had a big grin on her face.

"Peter, with your minor in public policy and minor in biology, teaching the Nest policy should be your job."

He shook his head. "You know, I jumped to that conclusion too. But really, lots of people can do the job. And Samantha and I are not on-site and have other commitments."

He turned to face Mark. "Are you interested? You're on-site, but it would mean a lengthy daily meeting."

"I'd be fine with meeting every day. But I know almost nothing about government. To teach something, you should know the subject well."

Jerry rolled his eyes. "No, many of my high school teachers didn't know their subject. They seemed to be learning it the day before they taught it."

Mark said, "I'm sad to hear your school didn't do right by you. But this is different. It would be a huge responsibility. We need someone who could do the job well."

I said, "You are right. We need the right person. It wouldn't be one *teacher* working on their own. It would be a mentor working as part of a team. I think attitude is more important than content mastery. What Jerry said about his teachers in high school learning material to teach it didn't mean they were bad teachers."

Jerry said, "Sam is right. Some of them were great. They told us when they needed to dig information out for us."

Peter said, "If you're interested in being the on-site mentor, talk to Dr. Kelly about it. I would love to be part of the project. The subject is near to my heart. I could prepare lesson materials and select instructional videos instructing on topics."

"I forgot we use video communication now. I guess we could show instructions and videos. But we would still need someone who knows the subject and answer questions," Mark said.

"Peter, why not be the instructor? Couldn't you work it around your commitments?" Mom asked.

I reached over and took Peter's hand. "We have a very cool opportunity that will have us away from Coastal Eleven. So the timing is not good for it."

Mom tilted her head. "Okay, what kind of opportunity, and how far away?"

I said, "You know Alana is back from Australia after spending a year as a visiting scientist. Well, she said the head of the program suggested she talk to us about it. If we apply, they would likely offer us positions in the program."

Mom looked amused. "You want to go to Australia? Wasn't Cuba far enough?"

"Mom, it's the Great Barrier Reef. Alana says the octopuses live in groups. They are likely intelligent."

Mark said, "Let me play devil's advocate here for a minute. We have a robust community of intelligent octopuses on the Georgia reef, seeking to solidify their association with humanity and asking for mentors so they can have a voice in what the future holds for them and us. In Australia, they have octopuses who *might* be intelligent. Are you sure you want to center your efforts in Australia?"

His reasoning was sound, but missing something important. "Mark, turn it around. Here in Georgia, the work is going to happen. The process has started, and the NOAA team is strong and well-funded. In Australia, they haven't made a breakthrough. That's why they want us."

"It sounds like you've decided," Mom said.

"Maybe," I said.

Peter said, "We still need to talk to Dr. Kelly about Charlie's proposal. This project would represent a huge commitment. It will need his approval. Mark, should we say you are interested?"

"Yes, but share my concerns, and I would like to talk to him before he makes any final decisions."

"Sounds good. We must also talk to our program supervisors about the visiting scientist program. They might disapprove. But it's a good opportunity. I expect they will work a way out for us to incorporate the year abroad as part of our doctorate programs."

Mom didn't look distressed. She didn't even look resigned. She looked a bit proud. I guessed she was getting used to the fact that her daughter was a grownup now, and grownup kids went away and did their own thing. But I couldn't help but feel that Mark had much to do with her new attitude. She had more of her own life now that she had a partner again. Change had been good for all of us.

Chapter 7 ~ Charlie Mystery on the Reef

It had been two warm seasons without white coral. With no bleaching, there was no need to apply probiotic paste, and NOAA instructed us to perform a new task. I watched the Younglings carry a transport box and set it on the sand. Each Youngling pulled a tiny living coral fragment and placed it into an opening in the rock rubble along the edges of the reef.

The fragments multiplied. Some earlier pieces had formed impressive stone forests with new homes for fish and crabs. Hunting was rich, and our Brothers provided food for our members. We would have many Younglings survive this year.

We selected this location for its favorable traits and moved our Nest here. It was a good home for us and was even better now. Samantha said the new coral helped keep ocean water from warming, and her team at NOAA was pleased that our reef was growing larger.

I watched the Younglings work surrounded by parrot fish. Like most brightly colored fish, parrot fish tasted bad, and the Younglings ignored them. Samantha explained that the way these fish graze on algae kept the coral from being overgrown by algae. They seemed even more beautiful now that I knew they helped coral grow.

Samantha was my friend, but she had also been a mentor. Now, when I saw a fish, I thought of the *name* Samantha gave us for that fish. Samantha thought she taught us *human* names. She did not know naming was new to us. Humans had names for everything! At first, learning names was hard. It came easier now.

All the Brothers and Younglings were adopting names for each other, and many were learning the names of fish and coral. We never felt the need for names before, yet returning to not using them would be hard. I thought using names helped us process information and communicate. It made me wonder. *Do fish use names? Do they communicate? Do wild octopuses? And if they don't use language, is it because no one taught them or because they cannot?*

A Youngling from Runt's brood approached, pulling me away from my thoughts.

"There is something you should see," she messaged.

I followed her to the sand beyond the edge of the reef. I examined where the coral fingers extended from the dense coral wall into the sand. It was an area with patches of rock rubble, algae, some sponges, and sea fans. The rubble had coral fragments that had been lovingly positioned by the Younglings. Several were large enough to have tiny fish and crabs sheltering among them.

The water was clear, and sunlight moved across the rubble patch. Almost all the fragments had polyps extended and were feeding. This section would join the fringe of the reef, and we would one day have more feeding grounds. The humans would be pleased to see how well the work was progressing.

"Your brood is doing excellent work. These corals are thriving."

"We did not place these here."

I moved closer, examining the fragments, and saw what the Youngling wanted me to see. Among the branching corals were tiny brain and star corals. They were not large, but they, too, had polyps extended and were feeding. *How had they gotten here? These were not the types we distribute.*

"Did another brood of Younglings work in this area?"

"None of us work with the massive corals. And they are showing up in more of our patches. If we did not place them, how did they get here?"

"I do not know," I answered. "How many areas have these non-branching coral growths?"

"We are working on ten patches right now. Three of them have these corals. They are on the quiet side of the reef where water moves slowly."

"Are they in the lagoon sites?" I asked.

The Youngling paused, jetted over, and asked another brood member.

"Yes, but only in a few sites, not as many as here."

The new growth of massive corals was interesting. The new corals were slow-growing massive corals typical of what we called *old reefs*. I would talk to Mark about this. He might know where they came from and why they were spreading.

Chapter 8~ Samantha At NOAA

Coastal Eleven, Georgia, February 2047

I was fairly sure that if we applied for the visiting scientist's positions, we would get them, and I wasn't wrong. My acceptance email came in on August 3, and Peter's came two days later. I waited nervously for those two days. I didn't tell anyone but Peter about the news. We had decided not to accept if only one of us was invited. We were at Coastal Eleven and shared our news over dinner.

Dr. Kelly expected that we would be going and had planned to reshuffle our duties at Coastal Eleven. Our advisers at Georgia Tech had begun planning to shift our degree work online and to incorporate our work in Australia as part of our programs. We had to clear out our unit in married student housing and move our belongings into storage. It would have been embarrassing if we hadn't been accepted.

That was more than two months ago, and we were leaving in eight days. We took the ferry to New Savannah and gathered at the institute to discuss the details of the "education program" requested by Charlie and the Elders.

"Are you excited?" Dr. Kelly asked.

"We are," Peter and I said in unison. Then we all laughed.

We decided that Mark would start a schedule of two instructional meetings per week. Peter had the first months' lessons ready for delivery and would begin working on additional lessons while we traveled. With twenty days on a ferry, he felt he could get a lot done.

What was the saying? Necessity the mother of invention? Well, our "needs" lit a fire under the Georgia Tech Artificial Intelligence team. They developed an octopus avatar that would "talk" to Charlie and Runt. It was unnerving to watch. The simulation was projected onto the advanced communication mat and integrated into an underwater scene. It even included fish swimming in the background. Watching it operate as I typed a message in nearly blew my mind.

"How do you like S.A.M.?" the AI specialist asked at the end of the demonstration.

"Why S.A.M.? Does that stand for something?" I could hear ill-suppressed laughter around the room, and Dr. Kelly was turning red. Suspicion was growing, and I didn't like it.

"No," I said. "Please tell me S.A.M. isn't short for Samantha."

"Well, technically its an acronym for Speaking Aquatic Mime, but, yeah, it's short for Samantha."

I decided not to make a fuss. It was kind of funny.

The demonstration left me with a feeling that this development would be important. It would exponentially improve the ability to communicate with the Nest. I wondered if we could eventually use the system for distance communication. Might Zoom meetings with octopuses one day be possible?

As usual, we had a manpower shortage on Coastal Eleven. Mark couldn't dive on his own to deliver the lessons. We needed a second diver available for a twice-a-week meeting and someone to run the boat and keep an eye on the divers when they were underwater. Mom and Mark were the only ones on the island full time. Mom wasn't certified for the use of scuba, but she could run the boat.

There were lots of volunteers, but we wanted people who knew and could step right into the project. We didn't want to risk an unknown personality. Alana was certified and could free up her schedule to rotate two weeks at Coastal Eleven with two weeks in New Savannah at her lab.

Jerry asked to increase his involvement and rotate with Alana as the second diver. He pitched the idea of filming the instructional lessons to the Film Department at Georgia State. They worked with him to adjust the classes to be distance learning classes for the year. It meant his senior year would be heavy with science classes, but he was happy with the arrangement. It was a heavy responsibility for a teenager, but he had the experience and would be fine.

We had worked out the details for rotating coverage so Mark would have a dive partner. We enjoyed a social visit, and Peter and I pumped Alana for the details of her travel to Australia. The outlawing of all fossil fuels dramatically changed expectations for international travel. The trip to Cuba was complicated, but it was nothing compared to traveling to Australia, a trip that would include planes, trains, and boats.

Our trip would start with a flight from Atlanta to Houston, then a train from Houston to the Matamoros on the Mexican border, transfer trains, and across Mexico to the city of Manzanillo, a major port where we board the Pacific Ferry.

Three years ago, the United Nations opened two solar refueling stations at strategic mid-Pacific locations. Each station had a retrofit aircraft carrier surrounded by a floating armada of solar panels. When a ferry docks, a crane swapped out specialized shipping containers with spent batteries for fully charged ones. The ferry from Mexico to New Zealand took twenty days.

Once we made it to New Zealand, we would fly to Sydney and then to Brisbane. We would be traveling for twenty-three days. My head hurt thinking about it.

It was funny. The last time we went overseas, Peter and I traveled to a symposium in Cuba. We were kidnapped and spent a harrowing three months where we didn't know what would happen to us. So, when Alana first approached us with the idea, my immediate reaction was panic. But I also could see Peter was keenly interested. And it was the Great Barrier Reef! Who wouldn't want to go?

It didn't take time for my panic to fade. Really, the Cuba thing turned out okay in a ton of ways. I married Peter, and the Nest is thrilled to be building a relationship with the colony of octopuses on the reef off Cuba.

Learner, a young female octopus that Charlie mentored, was still on the Cuban reef, trying to "civilize" the Cuban octopuses. I was only half joking. She was horrified to find that they had no organization for their mating, and because of this, they were all very short-lived. She herself had to rebuff males who requested mating.

The work Learner was doing in Cuba might have been the most significant outcome of the Cuban debacle. Without mentoring from one generation to the next, cultural progress was limited. If Learner convinced the Cuban octopuses to develop a system of mentors, real progress would be made.

I hoped the trip *to* Australia would be uneventful. I'd had enough of dealing with crazy people. At least in Australia, our cell phones would work, and we wouldn't feel as cut off as we had in Cuba. And they spoke English.

Chapter 9 ~ Blue Octopus~Heron Reef

Heron Island, Great Barrier Reef Australia

Sunlight streaked through the still waters of the lagoon, giving iridescent color to the corals that blanketed the flat area at the edge of Heron Reef. Life was everywhere. Fish of all sizes and colors darted between corals and sponges, feeding on their unlucky prey. The corals were also feeding, with their tiny coral polyps reaching into the water, gathering food.

On the reef's edge, a blue octopus moved along the sand, walking on his tentacles and inspecting his surroundings. He crossed between stands of coral, prodding the sand to locate hidden occupants and systematically snaring the unwary crab or small fish that failed to note the danger before it was too late. He had been quite successful and was no longer hungry but still explored.

In the distance, divers entered the water from a floating object. They swam down to the reef close to where the octopus rested. He observed the visitors. The creatures were large enough to trigger an urge to hide. But the octopus had seen them before. They seemed uninterested in hunting for food and had brought tasty crabs to share. So, he waited to see what they would do.

The divers moved to a sandy patch on the reef's edge and unrolled a mat covering a small section of sand. The three moved off to one side, and colors moved across the flat object covering the sand. A flash of green gave way to orange, yellow, and then blue.

The octopus moved closer. The sequence of colors was like those used for communication with his hunting companions. He looked around to see if another octopus was in the area. There were none. He looked again at the strange creatures. Moving closer, he used tentacles to respond to the strange beings with his own sequence, which said he was ready to cooperate in hunting.

One creature moved toward him, offering a crab. He took the crab, allowed his ridges to relax, and used a sequence of blue and green in his tentacles to message that he appreciated the food. While he had his snack, one of his hunting partners, a larger male octopus, approached.

His companion looked at the remnants of the crab scattered on the sand, and said, *"They presented you with food."* It wasn't a question, but the octopus could tell his hunting partner was curious.

"They sometimes bring food. I think it is an effort to keep me interacting with them."

The large male seemed surprised. *"Why?"*

"I don't know. But they present colors. I think they might be trying to send a message."

"Lots of creatures present colors. Only we send messages."

"Are you sure? Watch."

He moved toward the visitors and allowed his ridges to pulse. Then moving pieces of coral rubble and using the customary sequence of colors, he composed a message. *"We greet you, visitors to our reef."* Then he waited, looking at his companion.

While the strange visitor responded by sending the exact sequence of colors dancing across the sand.

"They use colors, but they have no meaning."

"Can we be sure? And, should we be this close, they might be dangerous."

The smaller octopus responded, *"I have not seen them hunt on the reef.*

I do not even know what they eat."

"See? We don't know what they eat. We should stay farther away."

"They will leave soon. They have been here before. I expect they will go up to the air soon. They have been down a long time."

"Even the whales do not stay down in water this long."

One of the strange creatures examined the coral pattern from the larger octopus. He moved to a clear area of sand and arranged rock fragments and coral rubble into a similar pattern. When he was done, colors moved across the flat object they had laid on the sand.

"It is obvious they are intelligent and are trying to communicate with us. Have you brought this to our senior family?"

The strangers rolled up the device from the sand and rose into the water. They reached the surface and disappeared from view. Soon, a shadow moved across the sand. The octopuses looked upward and watched the object move away from the reef and disappear in the distance.

"We should find out from the seniors if others have seen these creatures."

"Agreed."

Chapter 10~ Samantha~To the Far Side of Earth

Atlanta, Georgia, 2047

"You know, Australia is as far as you can travel from here. It's literally on the other side of the world."

Sheri was my best friend from college, and I loved her, but she was overly dramatic.

"You know me. I'm an overachiever."

She laughed, and Peter came in from the kitchen with a bottle of white wine.

"Anyone ready for a top-up?"

"Yes," Sheri and I said in unison.

Then we burst out laughing. We hadn't been able to visit in person much since graduation, and I hated that. The internet helped. We texted and sent each other links to important things. But I missed the connection we had when we shared a dorm room. I missed actually seeing her. College was funny that way. I majored in zoology, and Sheri majored in mechanical engineering. We had almost nothing in common, which didn't matter.

I graduated before Sheri. Her program was a five-year master's in civil engineering. Then, she took a job with the city, planning the network of moving sidewalks, scooters, bikes, and trams. Her team was responsible for maintaining a system that made it possible for people to move around in the large urban city that Atlanta had become.

The first time Mom visited Atlanta, she stayed for five days visiting museums and catching shows. She marveled at the transport system. You could get to every part of the city and only needed to walk a block or two at most. And Sheri helped keep the system working. Her team stayed incredibly busy. But tonight, she was making time to visit, and it was like old times when we were lived together.

Her apartment was a lot nicer than ours. City engineers must make a good living. She also put out an impressive spread of cheese and wine out for us. Maybe I should have studied engineering.

Peter raised a glass and toasted, "To a safe journey."

"To a safe journey," Sheri and I joined in.

"Samantha, can you do me a favor?" Sheri asked.

"Anything. What's up?"

"When your boat exchanges battery packs at Radiant Station. Can you take a video for me?"

"Can't you find them online?" Peter asked.

"No good ones. I've tried and can't see the details."

"I'll see what I can do," I said.

We had done some serious damage to the platter on the table and had just about emptied the second bottle of wine.

Peter said, "Sheri, isn't this outside what you work with? It's not like we need Radiant Station technology here in Atlanta."

"Not now, but who knows in the future?"

I looked at Sheri, remembering endless evenings in our old dorm at Georgia Tech, talking about the challenges of transportation in the post–fossil fuel world. I knew she would be interested, even if it weren't immediately applicable.

I was six years old in 2035. It was a pivotal year. Coastal flooding, mudslides, and massive storms cost the world over a billion people. At the end of the year, close to a third of all coastal cities were underwater. Every nation on earth was impacted. Governments banned fossil fuels in a desperate effort to stem climate collapse.

Shelter, water, and food were the immediate concern. I could say from experience that once you lived in a climate refuge camp, sleeping in tents, you understood that the world had changed. It took time, but within two years, the fear of floods and climate catastrophe became less pressing and people started long-term planning.

As they rebuilt the coastal cities in less vulnerable lands, they took pains to plan for local food sources. Community farms and hydroponic centers were dispersed to make transporting food easier. They needed to provide energy and transportation. Energy was the key to everything, and that meant an earnest expansion of solar, wind, geothermal, and nuclear power plants. The retooling of the energy system was an ongoing process. But, nothing was off the table other than a return to fossil fuels.

Providing food and water required reworking transportation to move supplies and to get people supplies they needed to go. High-speed electric trains were already in place in parts of the country. The engineers were given almost unlimited freedom and resources to improve and expand the rail network and reconnect most parts of the country. There were some electric cars in use, but the engineers dismissed the idea of replacing all cars with electric. They showed that widespread personal vehicles consumed too much energy for sustainability. We had electric vans and cars, but they were limited to official use in areas where other transport was simply not usable.

Two years after the flood, life began to find a new normal. People needed to move between where they lived, worked, shopped, and studied. It was the golden age of public transportation. Moving sidewalks, electric trains, bicycle stations, and walking became a part of life after the great flooding.

But the answer to travel between distant cities and countries would take longer. We had electric planes now, but they were small and limited by the size and weight of electric batteries. They could hop between close cities, but two hours in the air was the limit. Boat travel needed to be overhauled as well.

Sheri's interest was reasonable, and I should have expected it. This was the next big challenge: reinventing cross-pacific travel. The goal was to reconnect cities and countries by converting plane and ship travel to use batteries powered by solar systems or other renewable energy solutions. It was a big task.

It would take Peter and me just over three weeks to travel to Brisbane. But that the trip was possible at all was a modern miracle of human ingenuity.

The conversation drifted to local politics, something I was not interested in, but Peter had strong opinions. Pulling myself back into the now, I tried to pick up enough of the conversation thread to mask that I'd not been listening.

Sheri smiled, looked at me, and pulled an envelope out of her bag. She handed it to me.

"What is it?" I asked.

"Glad to have you back with us," she said, smiling. "It's a request to allow you to take video recordings of the battery transfer process."

I opened the envelope and read the message. "This should help me get up close. Thanks for thinking of it."

"I told my boss you'd be okay with it," she said with a huge smile.

I nodded. "Of course we are."

"I know it isn't a big interest for you, but it is for me, and I appreciate it."

Peter said, "I'm interested. The process is mind-blowing."

"I'm interested too. What made you think I wouldn't be?"

"Samantha, sometimes, it felt like all you thought about was coral reefs." She looked at Peter, then back at me. "I think Peter is having a good influence on you."

I felt myself turning red. "Peter is working on expanding my interests, or maybe I'm just growing up. But truly, I am interested in the solar station, and I will be more than happy to make observations and take pictures."

"Sam, I'm going to miss you. I can't believe you're going away for a whole year."

I got up and hugged her. "I'm going to miss you, too."

Chapter 11 Samantha ~ Heron Island

Heron Island, Australia, March 2047

As I looked over the white sand and turquoise water, it hit me that our travel was over. We would repeat it going home, but for now, *travel was over*. We left Atlanta six weeks ago. "It's not the destination; it's the journey." I understood what people meant by that saying because it was a fantastic journey: trains, planes, and boats. It felt decadent to spend twenty days on a vessel crossing the Pacific.

Oh, we worked. Peter planned lessons for Mark to deliver to the Nest and researched the public policy brief he was writing. I wrote two papers and planned the first few lectures I'd deliver at the University of Queensland. But we enjoyed walks on the deck, sunrise and sunset, and meals in the galley, where we met people from all over the world.

We spent our first two weeks in Australia at the University of Queensland, learning about research programs and the geography of the reef. It made me antsy. What I wanted was to get out and see the reef. *Would it be anticlimactic by the time we made it to Heron Island?*

It was not. Once they cleared us for the field station, we took the Gladstone train and the ferry to Heron. Now, we're eighty kilometers off the coast of Queensland on a coral cay surrounded by a reef flat and lagoon.

From where I stood, I could see the reef crest and the open sea beyond.

The sight left me feeling seriously isolated from the rest of the world.

I didn't mind the isolation. Heron was like Coastal Eleven but different enough to be fascinating. Our morning walk circumnavigated the island in an unhurried forty-five-minute walk. The small island had a harbor on one end and a sand spit on the other, and we walked in the early morning while the temperature was cool.

My forty-five-minute estimate didn't include the inevitable delays, like stopping to watch a turtle lumber up the beach to lay eggs or a stop to watch a blacktip reef shark cruise the shallow water right off the beach. It didn't include the mandatory pause to watch the sunrise. We were here to work but made time to enjoy the island.

Our cabin was in a thick strand of Pisonia trees near the island's center. The thick, lush vegetation hosted crested shearwaters, known in Australia as "muttonbirds," nesting in underground burrows. We used flashlights in early, dark mornings to avoid stepping into the nest holes—bad for us and the birds.

When muttonbirds called to each other, they sounded like they were moaning. It gave the tropical "forest" an almost haunted vibe. In the open air, these birds were magnificent fliers. They soared and glided effortlessly. But they were so clumsy near the ground they sometimes flew right into people. Not that it ever happened to me. Yeah, they were bizarre birds.

Our cabin in the woods didn't have a kitchen. None of the cabins had kitchens. The island administration built a communal kitchen and meal hall to encourage communication and research collaboration over meals. Conversations in the research laboratory or the field continued over food prep time and during meals. It was a sound system.

We were later than usual this morning, and the kitchen was almost empty.

"Good morning," Bill said, raising his coffee as if he were saluting and pointing to a plate of blueberry scones on the table.

Bill was a tall lanky red head with freckles. He had to be careful of the intense sun and wore a full "rash guard" and broad hat almost all the time. He was cheerful, and fun to work with.

We helped ourselves to one each and settled in to eat.

Peter took a bite and nodded appreciatively. "Who baked?" he asked.

"Sally, she made me promise to guard them until you got here so that you would get some."

I took a bite. Scones are like biscuits, but denser, slightly sweeter, and crunchy. Sally made these with heavy cream, nuts, and raisins. They were delicious.

Sally Martin, a pharmacology professor, had appointed herself my surrogate mother. I liked Sally, but she seemed too interested in ensuring I was eating enough. I had a reputation for missing meals that went back to childhood, and I could admit I was too skinny. There were advantages to her mothering. Sally was an excellent cook, and I rarely turned down her goodies.

Peter poured us coffee and sat beside me, taking an appreciative bite of his scone.

"Bill, I'd like to ask about the buildings on Heron."

"What do you want to know?"

"Some of your buildings are new, and some look ancient. I'd love to know the history."

"The oldest buildings date back to the turtle canning facility in the 1920s, but not much of the original buildings are still standing."

"People caught and ate turtles?" I asked.

Bill nodded. "They canned the meat and collected the body fat for furniture and car wax. They just about wiped all the turtles out, and the cannery closed. After that, investors modified the buildings and opened a tourist resort."

"That's not the one here now?" Peter asked.

"Yes and no. When it opened, it was just a few wooden shacks, and they shipped in food and water from the mainland. But the island was surrounded by a spectacular reef. A steady stream of tourists came for the fishing, snorkeling, and diving. They kept the primitive resort filled. Over time, the cottages have been rebuilt and replaced—until today, it is a modern and aesthetic resort."

"And the research station?" I asked.

"In 1943, the Australian government added a research station. That was when the government included Heron Reef as part of the national park system."

I looked at the room we were sitting in, noting it looked modern. "When was this building added?"

"The original station was one big room. Researchers slept on cots and put them away to work during the day. Much of what you see now was built by the University of Queensland in 1970 when they partnered with the government to upgrade the station. They hired an administrator, expanded the research laboratory rooms, and built cabins for scientists. After a fire in 2007, the university rebuilt and added a solar panel farm and a reverse osmosis water system. Cyclones and flooding meant periodic repairs and some rebuilding, but the research station and the resort remain."

"They'll be waiting for me in the lab. Thanks for the history lesson. It's fascinating."

"Glad to be of help," he said.

Peter said, "Sam, I'll be in the library for a few hours."

"Working of curriculum for Charlie and Runt?"

"Yes, I'm trying to prepare a template for individual lessons and a topic scope and sequence so Dr. Keller can start having other people draft lessons."

"That will be good. You don't want to spend all your time in the library. See you at lunch. Love you."

"Love you too," he said as I headed out the door.

The rhythm of island life works for me: lab work in the morning and fieldwork on the reef in the afternoon. Sometimes, we went to the reef flat and took measurements of new coral colonies growing under controlled conditions in lab aquariums. It sounded like what we had done in Georgia, but the Australians learned from our mistakes and changed how they approached the work.

In America, we went for fast-growth corals. It made sense since our goal was maximum reef growth for the absorption of carbon dioxide. But our approach lowered coral diversity over time as fast-growing corals out-compete the slower ones. Losing diversity can make a habitat prone to collapse if environmental factors place unusual stress on the system. The result could be a large-scale loss of individuals and species.

When the Nest selected reef areas for colonization, they looked for what they called *old* reefs. They couldn't express the science behind ecological stability, but they knew what made an area "good hunting" for long periods.

Australians had even more at stake than Americans. The Great Barrier Reef contained over 3,000 individual reefs spanning 2,300 km off the northern Queensland coast. Coral diversity in this system dwarfed what we had in the Atlantic. They knew our approach, using bio-engineered fast-growing corals, would lower the diversity of coral on the reef. For a while, it seemed like every scientist in Australia was working on reef biology, and they came up with a novel approach. Instead of genetically engineering corals, they developed new strains of the symbiotic algae found in every reef-building coral.

They depended on genetic engineering, but now they were modifying the symbiotic algae, zooxanthellae, to resist being expelled when high temperatures stressed the corals. They seeded lab-grown corals with engineered zooxanthellae, then transplanted the corals to the reef and watched as the zooxanthellae spread to wild corals of every species.

Brilliant.

The question of how quickly and extensively the modified zooxanthellae colonized wild corals had not been determined. My team had been assigned to the task. We were taking bore samples from reef corals, isolating zooxanthellae, and taking them back to the lab, where we ran a polymerase chain reaction (PCR) to increase the amount of DNA to study, and then tested for gene markers found on the genetically modified algae.

Peter wasn't part of the lab team. He had his work for the mornings. But we worked together most afternoons collecting test samples. On other days, we went to the reef slope, making observations and video recordings of the local blue octopus. Being on the reef, work or not, was a treat. Heron had a much larger reef flat than Coastal Eleven, and the diversity of corals nearly blew our minds away.

Chapter 12 ~ Charlie ~ Learner Returns

Coastal Eleven Barrier Reef

It was early morning when I came upon Learner. Mark and Jerry told me Captain John was bringing her back, but I missed the release. I saw her nestled at the deep end of the lagoon among soft corals and sea fans. A storm had passed at night, leaving the area dark with turbid water. Her colors were dark, and her movements were uneven and uncertain. Somehow, she looked much older than I remembered from our travels in Cuba. *Have I aged that much, too?*

We did not know why Learner asked for transportation home now. We expected her to stay until our brood season was completed. She gave no reason for the early request, and while she answered the Elders' questions, they felt she was holding something back. As her mentor and friend, the Council asked me to press her for answers.

"I greet you, Learner. It is good you are home."

She responded, *"I am happy to be back in my Nest."*

"Learner, what happened that you came home so suddenly? "

Learner's movements slowed, and her colors darkened to almost black. *"I was learning their language, and that was all good. I am fluent now. But I was also learning their ways, which are very different from ours. At first, it was interesting, but the longer I stayed, the more I was drawn into their Nest structure. It was time to come home. I had accomplished my* work."

I adjusted my colors, using calm but encouraging pink and light purple hues. *"I am glad to have you home. You left a gap, and I've missed you. Many of us wondered if you would remain in Cuba. Your sudden request for transport surprised the Counsel. They asked me to find out if something happened."*

"I will try to explain, but it is difficult. The Cuban Nest does not raise broods the way we do. They form brood pairs, and the female does not eat the male. The female dies after the Younglings emerge from the eggs. The male persists long enough to see that his brood can hunt. Then he too dies."

"They reproduce like the wild octopuses here?" I asked.

"Yes."

"Do they have Elders?"

"They have some nonbreeding members who live longer, but it seems random. They do not select who reproduces."

An idea formed in my head, and I thought I understood why Learner asked to be brought home.

"Were they asking if you would reproduce?"

"Yes. It took me a while to understand that a male spending time with me was 'courting.' He was becoming persistent. My work with communication was complete. NOAA has a translation program now. It was time for me to come home."

"As Samantha would say, 'different places have different cultures.' We are glad to have you home."

Learner shifted, and her colors lightened to blue and then green. *"While their ways are different, the experience made me think about how we select Brothers for reproduction."*

"What are your thoughts?" I asked.

Her colors shifted to pink as she asked, *"Have the Elders selected any wild broods for reproduction?"*

"I don't know. I don't think so. We only select three Mothers for

reproduction each season."

"I understand, but if the traits that make me and others raised from wild octopuses are valuable, these traits will be lost if the Elders never select from the wild brood."

"Learner, we can bring this to the Elder Council, but remember, since we collect wild octopus eggs every season, we always add these traits to the Nest."

Learner paused before answering, "I will think about this. When I realized the male was seeking to have me reproduce, it left me confused. While I had no desire to reproduce, there was a feeling of honor as well. It made me think about how we select and honor breeding. I hope one day the Nest will give this honor one of my kind."

"I am sure we will select from a wild brood. But Learner, Younglings from wild eggs are still rare in our Nest, and Mothers die soon after laying eggs. We would have been sad to lose you. The time will come when one will be selected for reproduction."

"I understand. For now, it is good to be home and among friends. I want to rejoin the work with the wild broods the next time."

"There will be hatchlings soon, and I am sure they will gladly assign you a brood. Do you wish to be part of the Elder Council that selects for mating? I am sure they would value your input."

"Would they?" she responded.

"Yes. Why would the Council not?" I asked.

"I don't know. Being away and exposed to a different way of life made me question many things. Right now, I feel unsure of myself. It might be best not to make important decisions for a while."

I said, *"Take as much time as you need. Again, welcome home."*

Learner messaged a thank you and signaled that she would leave and find a place to rest. Our meeting was good for her. As she left, her colors were lighter, less burdened, and her motions were almost smooth.

Chapter 13 ~ Samantha ~ Telecommunication

Heron Island, Australia

Everyone was quick to assure us we would be dying to get back to "civilization" by the time our first rotation of fieldwork was over. But, I grew up on a barrier island. Isolation was normal.

Heron Island wasn't even primitive. The island had solar power, lovely private cottages with ceiling fans, and garden seating. We even had reliable internet. While we didn't have private bathrooms in the cottages, the shower house had hot water and was centrally located. The communal kitchen was better equipped than our place in Atlanta and certainly more modern than what I'd grown up with. *What were they missing?* The island was exotic and the reef spectacular. I figured the month would pass quickly.

I worried that Peter was not as taken with being there. He had a split appointment between the University of Queensland and NOAA, and that was like having two full-time jobs. Mostly he worked on research and lesson prep in the mornings for NOAA, and fieldwork with us in the afternoon. But he hadn't reached a good balance and looked frazzled leaving the lab.

"Everything okay?" I asked.

He was so preoccupied, he hadn't seen me catch up to him on the path to the cottage.

"Do you mind if I skip this afternoon's dive? Alana and Jerry say Charlie and Runt are devouring the information and are pushing for more."

"No problem. If it's an uneven number, I'm sure I can tag along with Jim and Evan."

"Thanks."

Peter was my dive partner for the afternoon dives, a practice that gave me a comfortable feeling of familiarity. I missed him when he was not with us for the afternoon work, particularly when we were diving.

It was hard to explain. The Australian locals knew the reef and water conditions, the dive gear we used, and the layout and operation of the boat. I was a junior team member without responsibilities for operational decisions. And my lack of input made me uncomfortable. Diving was a big part of my work. Usually, it was an activity I loved. But here in Australia, it was also my most significant source of stress. Some of the locals had different attitudes about diving safety than I did.

Back home, rule number one of diving was leaving at least one person on the boat at all times. That person tracked the position of divers in the water. As a teenager, I tied my boat off the reef crest and dove alone. One night, my boat came loose, and I ended up swimming in from the reef crest after dark. It was terrifying. Understandably, I felt rule number one should never be broken.

But these particular Australians didn't seem to agree about the need for a boat safety official and seemed casual about staying close to dive partners. I didn't think this was true of all Australians. They had a well-written official set of safety standards, but some Australians resisted regulations on principle. They only followed rules that they decided mattered. I couldn't say anything about it. I was a visiting researcher, still a "visitor." It was not my place to criticize. So, I wasn't looking forward to a dive without Peter. I was spoiled and like having a partner

I could count on to stay with me and not wander off.

We had two hours before our scheduled dive, so I dropped by the equipment shed to pick up tanks and check in with Jim and Even. They were sorting through electronics and camera equipment.

Jim and Evan were Australian graduate research assistants working at the research station full time. Jim was from central Queensland. He had a strong Aussie accent and sprinkled his conversation with colorful slang. Nobody seemed to mind or even notice. I often wished I had a translation program, but sometimes, when I did know what he was saying, I was embarrassed. So, maybe not having a translation program was a good thing.

Evan was from Melbourne in Victoria. His accent was more refined, and he didn't use as many alarming expressions as Jim. Well, a bit less. You got used to it after a while.

"Hi, Peter can't join us for the afternoon dive. Do you guys mind if I'm your third?"

Jim said, "No worries, luv. What's Peter up to?"

"Preparing lessons on government and history."

Both Jim and Evan didn't say anything for a while. They looked at me and then at each other.

"Yer kiddin', right?" Evan asked, eventually.

"Nope. Ask Peter about it at dinner. I'm sure he will talk your ears off." I didn't feel up to explaining.

Mark and Alana would deliver Peter's lessons to the octopuses. That just sounded too weird.

"No worries. We're all going to be in the same area."

I didn't say anything. I was part of the problem. Our task today was sampling coral for zooxanthellae. But, I was always on the lookout for signs of a blue octopus colony. If I came across something interesting, I would want to investigate. If I actually crossed paths with one or more octopuses, I would want to stay, watch, and possibly try to make contact. Peter was used to my way of work. He would stay by my side. It wasn't fair to expect Jim and Evan to follow my lead. They wanted to get samples and get out.

I'd been on dives with Jim and Evan. Yes, they tended to disappear if I didn't work to keep up with them. It shouldn't be a big deal. I was a big girl and could watch out for myself. After all, I had spent countless days wandering around a reef alone. In a way, these guys reminded me of my former confident self. It might be time to look for a new balance of caution and confidence.

I looked at the equipment Evan was sorting through. "Is that some kind of camera equipment?" I asked.

He nodded. "Yeah, we're gonna try it out today. The integrated computer program and motion detector keep the camera focused on a selected object. We trigger the program once we find an octopus we are interested in. The lens system will self-adjust to keep that subject in focus."

"I thought you guys were just collecting samples today."

"That was what we thought too, but Dr. Snyder called it in. We're your support today."

"Wow, I hope you don't mind."

"Yeah, no, luv, all reef time is a good time, and your octopus project sounds almost surreal."

"I know what you mean. I'm used to it, but talking to outsiders is hard. Most people think I'm crazy."

"I bet they do, silly buggers."

"You know, your equipment looks really impressive. But, you have to be on the reef to work it. Why not just designate a camera operator to do the job?"

Evan laughed. "That's what I bloody well said."

Jim said, "I don't think the silly buggers trust us."

I laughed and wondered what Jerry would think about the automated camera system. *Would he be out of a job?* I didn't think so. I trusted Jerry more than a machine. Then again, he might like it. A camera that kept a subject in focus would be helpful.

Jim said, "Evan is pullin' yer leg. We use a cameraman. The computer assist is to make our cameraman more effective and allow him to multitask on-site. Even if he tries to stay right on the subject, some of the video has a fair amount of out-of-focus imaging."

Now I knew Jerry would be interested in this technology

"Interesting. Our cameraman hasn't said it was a problem, but I bet he would be interested in any technology to improve his camera work." I wondered how Jerry would feel if he heard me refer to him as our cameraman.

"I'll meet you at the boat," I said and headed to my room to change.

I put on a suit and a rash guard. As I went to leave, Peter walked in.

He smiled, wrapping his arms around me. "Did you find a replacement diver for this afternoon?"

"Jim and Evan are okay with me tagging with them. Actually, Dr. Snyder put them on octopus duty."

"Good, make sure you stay with them. You know the Aussies aren't big on the whole dive buddies concept. Well, those two aren't, anyway."

"We'll be fine. But I'm glad Dr. Snyder adjusted their focus away from coral sampling. We're visiting the site of a blue octopus colony. If we find some, I'll try out the translation sequences from the Georgia Tech language guru. It's a testing afternoon. Jim and Evan want to try out new computer-assisted video equipment."

"Sounds like fun. You're making me sorry I'll miss the dive."

"I'll have more fun than you. I know working in the library and putting lessons together isn't fun, but it's important." I picked up my dive bag and headed for the door. "Don't work too hard. I'll see you when we get back."

"Have fun and stay safe," he called as the door shut behind me.

Above me, the sky was a vivid blue, not a cloud in sight. The air temperature was eighteen degrees Celsius, just cool enough to make a person feel alive and filled with energy. I was going to the harbor to take a pontoon boat for a reef dive. Life didn't get much better than this.

When I reached the boat, the other six divers were waiting. The jewel-blue water was as smooth as glass. A wave of excitement pushed my anxiety away.

Chapter 14 ~ Samantha ~ Reef Dive

Heron Island, Australia

Everyone was quick to assure us we would be dying to get back to "civilization" by the time our first rotation of fieldwork was over. But, I grew up on a barrier island. Isolation was normal.

Heron Island wasn't even primitive. The island had solar power, lovely private cottages with ceiling fans, and garden seating. We even had reliable internet. While we didn't have private bathrooms in the cottages, the shower house had hot water and was centrally located. The communal kitchen was better equipped than our place in Atlanta and certainly more modern than what I'd grown up with. *What were they missing?* The island was exotic and the reef spectacular. I figured the month would pass quickly.

I worried that Peter was not as taken with being there. He had a split appointment between the University of Queensland and NOAA, and that was like having two full-time jobs. Mostly he worked on research and lesson prep in the mornings for NOAA, and fieldwork with us in the afternoon. But he hadn't reached a good balance and looked frazzled leaving the lab.

"Everything okay?" I asked.

He was so preoccupied, he hadn't seen me catch up to him on the path to the cottage.

"Do you mind if I skip this afternoon's dive? Alana and Jerry say Charlie and Runt are devouring the information and are pushing for more."

"No problem. If it's an uneven number, I'm sure I can tag along with Jim and Evan."

"Thanks."

Peter was my dive partner for the afternoon dives, a practice that gave me a comfortable feeling of familiarity. I missed him when he was not with us for the afternoon work, particularly when we were diving.

It was hard to explain. The Australian locals knew the reef and water conditions, the dive gear we used, and the layout and operation of the boat. I was a junior team member without responsibilities for operational decisions. And my lack of input made me uncomfortable. Diving was a big part of my work. Usually, it was an activity I loved. But here in Australia, it was also my most significant source of stress. Some of the locals had different attitudes about diving safety than I did.

Back home, rule number one of diving was leaving at least one person on the boat at all times. That person tracked the position of divers in the water. As a teenager, I tied my boat off the reef crest and dove alone. One night, my boat came loose, and I ended up swimming in from the reef crest after dark. It was terrifying. Understandably, I felt rule number one should never be broken.

But these particular Australians didn't seem to agree about the need for a boat safety official and seemed casual about staying close to dive partners. I didn't think this was true of all Australians. They had a well-written official set of safety standards, but some Australians resisted regulations on principle. They only followed rules that they decided mattered. I couldn't say anything about it. I was a visiting researcher, still a "visitor." It was not my place to criticize. So, I wasn't looking forward to a dive without Peter. I was spoiled and like having a partner I could count on to stay with me and not wander off.

We had two hours before our scheduled dive, so I dropped by the equipment shed to pick up tanks and check in with Jim and Even. They were sorting through electronics and camera equipment.

Jim and Evan were Australian graduate research assistants working at the research station full time. Jim was from central Queensland. He had a strong Aussie accent and sprinkled his conversation with colorful slang. Nobody seemed to mind or even notice. I often wished I had a translation program, but sometimes, when I did know what he was saying, I was embarrassed. So, maybe not having a translation program was a good thing.

Evan was from Melbourne in Victoria. His accent was more refined, and he didn't use as many alarming expressions as Jim. Well, a bit less. You got used to it after a while.

"Hi, Peter can't join us for the afternoon dive. Do you guys mind if I'm your third?"

Jim said, "No worries, luv. What's Peter up to?"

"Preparing lessons on government and history."

Both Jim and Evan didn't say anything for a while. They looked at me and then at each other.

"Yer kiddin', right?" Evan asked, eventually.

"Nope. Ask Peter about it at dinner. I'm sure he will talk your ears off." I didn't feel up to explaining.

Mark and Alana would deliver Peter's lessons to the octopuses. That just sounded too weird.

"No worries. We're all going to be in the same area."

I didn't say anything. I was part of the problem. Our task today was sampling coral for zooxanthellae. But, I was always on the lookout for signs of a blue octopus colony. If I came across something interesting, I would want to investigate. If I actually crossed paths with one or more octopuses, I would want to stay, watch, and possibly try to make contact. Peter was used to my way of work. He would stay by my side.

It wasn't fair to expect Jim and Evan to follow my lead. They wanted to get samples and get out.

I'd been on dives with Jim and Evan. Yes, they tended to disappear if I didn't work to keep up with them. It shouldn't be a big deal. I was a big girl and could watch out for myself. After all, I had spent countless days wandering around a reef alone. In a way, these guys reminded me of my former confident self. It might be time to look for a new balance of caution and confidence.

I looked at the equipment Evan was sorting through. "Is that some kind of camera equipment?" I asked.

He nodded. "Yeah, we're gonna try it out today. The integrated computer program and motion detector keep the camera focused on a selected object. We trigger the program once we find an octopus we are interested in. The lens system will self-adjust to keep that subject in focus."

"I thought you guys were just collecting samples today."

"That was what we thought too, but Dr. Snyder called it in. We're your support today."

"Wow, I hope you don't mind."

"Yeah, no, luv, all reef time is a good time, and your octopus project sounds almost surreal."

"I know what you mean. I'm used to it, but talking to outsiders is hard. Most people think I'm crazy."

"I bet they do, silly buggers."

"You know, your equipment looks really impressive. But, you have to be on the reef to work it. Why not just designate a camera operator to do the job?"

Evan laughed. "That's what I bloody well said."

Jim said, "I don't think the silly buggers trust us."

I laughed and wondered what Jerry would think about the automated camera system. *Would he be out of a job?* I didn't think so. I trusted

Jerry more than a machine. Then again, he might like it. A camera that kept a subject in focus would be helpful.

Jim said, "Evan is pullin' yer leg. We use a cameraman. The computer assist is to make our cameraman more effective and allow him to multitask on-site. Even if he tries to stay right on the subject, some of the video has a fair amount of out-of-focus imaging."

Now I knew Jerry would be interested in this technology

"Interesting. Our cameraman hasn't said it was a problem, but I bet he would be interested in any technology to improve his camera work." I wondered how Jerry would feel if he heard me refer to him as our cameraman.

"I'll meet you at the boat," I said and headed to my room to change.

I put on a suit and a rash guard. As I went to leave, Peter walked in.

He smiled, wrapping his arms around me. "Did you find a replacement diver for this afternoon?"

"Jim and Evan are okay with me tagging with them. Actually, Dr. Snyder put them on octopus duty."

"Good, make sure you stay with them. You know the Aussies aren't big on the whole dive buddies concept. Well, those two aren't, anyway."

"We'll be fine. But I'm glad Dr. Snyder adjusted their focus away from coral sampling. We're visiting the site of a blue octopus colony. If we find some, I'll try out the translation sequences from the Georgia Tech language guru. It's a testing afternoon. Jim and Evan want to try out new computer-assisted video equipment."

"Sounds like fun. You're making me sorry I'll miss the dive."

"I'll have more fun than you. I know working in the library and putting lessons together isn't fun, but it's important." I picked up my dive bag and headed for the door. "Don't work too hard. I'll see you when we get back."

"Have fun and stay safe," he called as the door shut behind me.

Above me, the sky was a vivid blue, not a cloud in sight. The air temperature was eighteen degrees Celsius, just cool enough to make a person feel alive and filled with energy. I was going to the harbor to take a pontoon boat for a reef dive. Life didn't get much better than this.

When I reached the boat, the other six divers were waiting. The jewel-blue water was as smooth as glass. A wave of excitement pushed my anxiety away.

Chapter 15 ~Samantha~ Meeting Blue

Heron Island, Australia

Chris started the motor as I stepped on board. Silently, the boat pulled away from the pier, moved out of the harbor, and skirted the outer reef wall. I pushed my bag under our bench and settled in to enjoy the ride. The clear turquoise water looked cool and inviting, and my mind rehearsed the steps for today's dive.

When I glanced back at the steering platform, Chris looked annoyed and seemed to glare at me.

I asked, "Was I late?"

"No, you were on time, but we're watching a weather system on radar. It's best to get out for our dive without wasting time."

"You could have texted me to come early."

"No worries, mate. We're okay for time. Storm's a good way out."

Evan patted me on my shoulder. "Samantha, relax. You got here about one minute after I did."

"Okay, thanks."

We were heading to the area where Alana documented a small colony of *cyanea*, the blue octopus. The site was just off the reef wall, west of the island, a location with massive coral heads. Peter and I had visited to observe the colony. On the last visit, we used the display mat and presented a "greeting" in the Nest's language. The local octopuses watched the display, and one individual approached. He was attentive, with ridges erect—all signs of curiosity in octopuses. I was encouraged by his interest. *Did he recognize my sequence as an attempt to communicate? I wish I knew.*

I thought about my first encounter with Charlie. He had been watching me handle pieces of coral rubble and thought I was trying to communicate. He "responded" by manipulating coral rubble in front of me. That encounter began the octopus communication project and a friendship that shaped my life.

I'd worked so many hours with the software program developed at Georgia Tech, that I recognized patterns and could understand much of what Charlie said, even without the equipment. Of course, without equipment, I couldn't respond.

In Cuba, the octopuses used a similar means of communication, but the color sequences and tentacle movements differed. It appeared octopus populations had their local languages. So, we expected communicating here in Australia would require programming or adjusting the translation software.

Today, we would be field-testing S.A.M. (yes - "speaking aquatic mime" is lame, but I won't call the avatar Sam—that's my name). Mark and Jerry had been using the avatar extensively in the "history lessons" they were delivering. It made sense, as our communication mat was a very thin, flexible display monitor that we used to project color sequences. Recently, we redesigned the display mat so we could use it to show video to the octopuses. It was part of the Elders' request to learn more about human society. The high-definition resolution for showing videos led to the development of S.A.M, and the avatar proved to be an effective enhancement to cross-species communication.

Our results here in Australia without S.A.M. had been only so-so. We had the attention of the octopus colony. They watched us with interest, and my gut feeling was that, like the octopus colonies we worked with from Georgia and Cuba, this local population, *octopus cyanea*, was intelligent and had a language.

But so far, I had failed to establish meaningful communication. My attempts to use our existing translation program failed, and we were not surprised. We suspected this group would have their own language. I kept my disappointment under control. We succeeded in Georgia and again in Cuba. It would be a lot of work, but it would also be exciting and fun. I hoped the use of our avatar would jump-start the process.

I met Charlie when I was fourteen, and we lived on an island in Georgia. He was a young octopus watching me handle pieces of coral rubble. The octopuses used moving coral pieces as sign language, and he thought I was trying to convey a message.

Octopuses used a sophisticated system of tentacle motions, chromatophores to send sequences of color changes across their skin, and placement of coral rubble pieces on the sand to communicate with each other. We used machine language and artificial intelligence to refine translation software and hardware for the past six years. Our team could now communicate with Charlie's group using the equipment. And really, I'd spent so much time with electronic tentacle motion as part of our octopus language when delivering information or asking questions.

The sophisticated array of liquid crystals in the mat gave our avatar image an almost three-dimensional appearance. Charlie and the Elders had been slightly startled by S.A.M., but they quickly got used to our use of it. And using the avatar enhanced our communication greatly.

Today, I would try S.A.M. out with the Australian octopus population. My phone had the software to run the avatar program loaded and ready to use. The updated app used new sequences based on the video recordings Peter and I sent to Georgia Tech. The computer language experts loaded what they hoped was a greeting sequence. One of my dive partners, Evan, was excited about today's experiment. But Jim thought the idea was lame. I wished Peter were here. If my use of S.A.M. flopped, the ribbing would be fierce.

I hugged the display mat, rolled off the boat into the blue water, flipped over, and glided to the white sand below us. The sounds of two splashes told me that Evan and Jim had entered the water and were behind me. Our target was a hollowed-out massive coral head. It was a location blue octopuses seemed to favor. Hopefully, we would have some productive interactions.

A large school of grunts drifted around the coral head. They were so thick I couldn't see where the opening to the coral cave was. The grunts glared at me as I approached. These fish saw tourists snorkeling and diving so often they ignored us. They didn't even scatter. I was within arm's reach of them when the school parted for me.

A two-meter opening to a hollowed center was in the back of the massive coral head. I unrolled my display mat onto the sand directly before the cavernous opening and connected my phone to the mat.

Evan was three meters off to my right, setting up our camera equipment and waiting for the action. I activated the avatar application on my phone, triggering the display mat to project an image of a blue octopus that appeared on the mat. Our technical department adjusted the parameters so the image matched the color and look of the local species of octopus.

I adjusted the program directions, and S.A.M.'s tentacles began moving. Color sequences flashed across his head and arms. My dive partners had not seen the avatar in use. While they knew about the technology, they were visibly impressed. The graphics on the display mat were so good that S.A.M. took on an almost three-dimensional appearance. I had a hunch the local octopuses were here and watching us, and I hoped they would join us soon.

We had been using an avatar on my reef in Georgia. My octopus friend Charlie had been a bit spooked the first time he saw S.A.M. But, after the initial shock, they warmed up to using an avatar, and we all agreed that the projected octopus image enhanced communication. It made sense. Octopuses used tentacle movement and color sequences. Humans were at a disadvantage without tentacles. Using an avatar helped level the playing field. Mark and Jerry used the avatar to communicate with Learner in Cuba. We hoped using the avatar would make our job here in Australia easier.

The coral cave had a white sand floor. A tentacle appeared before me, and I pulled back, not wanting to spook the occupant. Soon, a blue octopus emerged, reaching a tentacle toward the mat with the avatar. I motioned to Jim, and he focused the camera on our visitor.

Optical fiber cables linked the camera, computer, phone, and display mat, providing super-fast data transfer rates. It was easy to forget the background technology. I talked into my microphone, and the avatar used octopus language to display my message. The camera analyzed the octopus's response and sent a vocal translation to my earpiece. The experience felt like I was talking to the octopus.

Right now, the responses were minimal. The more interactions we recorded and sent to the computer linguists for analysis, the more programmed vocabulary responses I would have to choose from.

I sent my first message, "Hello," and the avatar's tentacles moved gracefully to display the message.

My visitor moved to the center of the opening. He was small, only about ten centimeters across, and very blue. I watched as he darkened and moved his tentacles.

I heard a single word in my earpiece: "*What.*"

Was the software working? Maybe the Blue octopus had said, "*What?*"

I spoke into my microphone, "Hello, I greet you," to the tablet, and the avatar displayed a color sequence and tentacle motion to convey the message. Well, I hoped it conveyed the message. But Blue remained motionless. I called him Blue. He needed a name.

So, I tried another message. "My Elders greet you," and waited.

A second octopus moved out of the cave and joined Blue, settling off to the side and staring at the display mat. He was smaller than Blue, and I assumed he was a Youngling. He inched forward, but Blue pushed the Youngster to the side. His rapid color changes and pulsating ridges showed unease. Then Blue reached a tentacle out and stroked the surface of the mat. The avatar pulsed and stared back at him.

A third octopus moved out from the hollowed coral head to join us. The three octopuses were exchanging information. I wished I knew what they were saying. Hopefully, Jim was on camera recording the motions.

I hadn't thought this through. When I introduced the avatar to Charlie, he understood human technology and accepted the avatar as a machine. It might have been too soon to introduce the avatar.

Like Blue, another octopus came forward, reached with a tentacle, and stroked the mat. They all saw the image on the mat and reacted to it in a way that suggested they recognized it as an octopus. That recognition was important.

Blue's colors were lighter now. He was trying to piece the puzzle together. As I watched, he began moving his tentacles and sending a color sequence.

These days, I understood Runt, Learner, and Charlie enough to understand what they are discussing. But these tentacle motions were different enough that I had no idea what Blue was saying. His colors were dark and brooding, and the ridges on his skin were pulsing. My octopus visitor was agitated and distressed. My earpiece remained silent. The translation software could not process the information.

I tried again in calming colors and messaged, "Friend," then added "Brother."

Again, I watched as the small group of octopuses messaged each other. Then, there was an explosion of black ink, and when the water cleared, the octopuses were gone.

Jim's voice came sounded in my earpiece. "That was different."

"Indeed, it was. Were you able to record the conversation between the octopuses?" I asked.

"I did. Should we pack up? Will they return?"

"I've never had a meeting end with black ink, and I don't think it's a good sign. Let's pack this up. We'll try again tomorrow."

He and Evan packed the camera gear. I rolled the mat up and put the tablet into my bag. As we headed up to the boat, I did a final survey of the coral head, and there was not an octopus in sight.

Hopefully, their curiosity would balance their fear, and we would see them again.

Chapter 16 ~Blue~ Strange Creatures

We jetted away from the great coral head and sheltered in the reef slope. From the safety of the branching coral fingers, I watched the strange creatures gather objects and lumber away from where we witnessed the ghost octopus. My Younglings were dark and agitated. I urged them to shelter and still themselves as we watched the visitors rise into the water column and approach a shadow on the surface. One at a time, the three visitors disappeared from the water.

A feeling of balance returned to the reef after these strange creatures were gone. They came here often and seemed harmless. Most slow-moving creatures were not predators. But what I witnessed today was different and disturbing. *Had they captured one of us and held him captive in the sand?*

The strange ghost octopus *looked* as if he were composing a message. But the colors and motions conveyed no meaning. Maybe his capture left the poor creature insane, unable to think or communicate. I did not recognize the captive. He must not be from this reef. Maybe these visitors were not as harmless as we thought. The Elders must be warned. If this ghost was a captive, we must not allow them to capture anyone else. We needed a meeting. Maybe the Elders could make more sense of this disturbing event.

"Younglings," I signaled. *"Stay close and follow."* Leading my brood, we moved to deeper water. All seemed calm. A school of fish flowed

through a forest of sea fans and down the wall of the reef slope. The fish were aware of our presence. They moved about, keeping a safe distance from us. But I felt no sense from them that there were large predators nearby. It was not the time they usually hunted for food, but it was always important to be watchful. Reminding the Younglings to use caution in their movements, I led my group through the rock rubble and soft corals and into the entrance ahead of us.

An Elder approached as soon as we settled down among the sea fans and soft corals.

"Is something wrong?" he asked.

"We saw the slow-moving visitors today."

"They often come to the reef. Did they do something alarming?"

"Not alarming, but unusual and disturbing."

The Elder moved onto a sand patch between sea fans and sponges. Colors moved across his head and through his tentacles. *"Tell me what happened."*

"The visitors came from the surface. One spread something onto the sand. Then something happened, and a Brother appeared on the sand. He looked like he was trying to message, but it made little sense. The Brother did not look right. I tried to touch him. My tentacles passed through him as if he were not there."

"What do you mean he wasn't there?"

"I reached out and tried to connect. My tentacle reached right through him. I could see him but not touch him."

The Elder was still, deep in thought. Did he believe me? As if he read my mind, he addressed one of my Younglings.

"Did you see the captive Brother?" he asked.

"I did. It was just as my mentor described. We could see the Brother, but no one could touch him," the Youngling said.

The Elder turned to me, and our eyes met. *"It sounds like a most odd interaction. Was this the first time these visitors came to the reef?"*

We were attracting attention. There were now several Elders and Brothers gathering around us.

"These visitors have often come to the reef and never appeared dangerous. They have even brought us food. Today is the first time these visitors have brought this strange captive Brother. I do not know what to make of it."

I waited while the Elders exchanged ideas and information, wondering what they would have me do when the visitors returned. When they gave no response, I messaged.

"What do you suggest we do?" I asked.

"We should observe from a distance for a while. Maybe they will go away and we will not need to do anything."

"I think they had been trying to communicate," I motioned.

"Do not approach them again on your own. If we decide it is safe, I will come with you," the Elder signaled with colors blue and green.

Chapter 17 ~ Samantha~Little India

I loved being on the ocean with the early morning sun against my back and sitting next to Peter. It felt like a holiday. Dr. Snyder gave us the day off to run an errand for him in Gladstone, which was why we were on the ferry, but I still felt guilty.

"This is nice," I said. "I wonder if we'll see any whales."

"Maybe, although it's early in the year for them. It would be cool, but for now, I'm just enjoying the day off. And I'm looking forward to exploring Gladstone."

The water was deep blue, and the sun was still low in the sky, casting an orange glow on the horizon. We were both scanning the water for signs of whales.

It was warm but not hot. This was calving season, and if we were lucky, we might see some migrating. Heron Island was famous for them, and I'd never seen a whale.

"What does Dr. Snyder need us to do in Gladstone?" I asked.

"Go to the train station and pull the science supplies heading for Heron. He's expecting PCR primers, and the last time he ordered primers, they came in thawed, and he had to toss them out. Our job is to check the dry ice levels and repack the containers before bringing them to the ferry."

"And he gave us two days off just for that?"

"Well, I'm sure he figured it would allow us to see some of Australia."

"It is nice of him, but we'll have a tone of work to get caught up with.

"True, but our time here in Australia is limited. We've passed through Gladstone and never had time to explore. We can get caught up when we get back."

"You would think the people shipping the primers would pack enough dry ice for the trip!"

"I know. But I think it's a matter of how many people handle the package and, at each stage, how often the handling delays movement. The package is transferred between trains in Sydney, again in Brisbane, and once more between the train and ferry in Gladstone. If all the connections are made, the dry ice holds up fine. If one connection is missed, it might still be okay. If two connections are missed, the stuff arrives thawed and useless."

"I see your point, and the more dry ice they use, the larger the package and the more the shipping costs." I paused and then added, "But if I were Dr. Snyder, I would offer to pay more shipping and have the primers packed in a bigger freezer box with lots of dry ice. How could they object?"

"Good idea. Let's suggest that to Dr. Snyder."

We were sitting on the top deck, watching the coastline get larger and closer. We didn't see whales, but we saw turtles and dolphins. As we navigated the port, we watched in awe as we passed an endless procession of landing platforms with cranes and tall stacks of shipping crates. I pointed them out to Peter.

"This must be a huge center for shipping," I said

"Gladstone is a major commercial shipping port. It's the reason they couldn't move the city to a higher elevation inland. They need this port, and that means at least part of the city needs to stay directly on the coast, danger from flooding or not."

I walked to the railing and took a good look. As we passed one platform, I noted the large number of people at work and wondered how they might handle evacuations when coastal storms approach. Soon, the ferry was navigating into the port. We waited a few minutes for the boat to dock and tie up to the pier, grabbed our backpacks, and followed the other passengers off the boat. We were still on the pier when we heard a train whistle in the distance.

"Well," Peter said. "There's only one train, and it sounds like it's pulling in. Let's pick up dry ice and take care of the supplies now. Then we have the entire afternoon to explore."

"Sounds good," I said.

Walking on the street leading away from the port, vendors worked from carts. We passed flower carts, food vendors that smelled amazing, and others selling clothing. I walked over to a cart and admired a dress with a rich red fabric and gold thread woven into a pattern.

Peter saw me holding the dress. "It would look amazing on you," he said.

"I think so, too, but where would I wear it?"

"Sam, don't worry about that. I'll take you somewhere fancy back in Atlanta. It's a fusion of Indian fashion and modern Australian. It's unusual."

"Maybe on the way back tomorrow. I want to think about it."

"Look at the arrangement of carts and the buildings above them," Peter said.

"I see what you mean. When a storm moves in, the shopkeepers can move the inventory into the elevated buildings. Once the storm passes and the tide goes out, they can restock carts. Although they might need to replace carts."

"They might not need to replace them. Look, the carts have hitches in front and back. I bet they pull a caravan of the carts to a storage site at higher grounds."

"Smart," I agreed.

We made our way to a grocery store and picked up dry ice. The shop had a section for freshly baked pastries, and I bought two lamingtons, a sponge cake covered with chocolate and desiccated coconut. It was an impulse buy, but I love lamingtons and rarely had one. I slipped them into my backpack.

Half an hour later, we were at the train station, where Dr. Snyder's science supplies were located. We added five kilograms of dry ice to the Styrofoam shipping box with the sensitive biological supplies. The new dry ice would keep them frozen until they were safe in a freezer on Heron Island. We moved the packages to a locker at the ferry landing. We would pick them up in the morning when we were ready to board the boat for our return trip. It was noon, and we had finished our work for the day.

"Let's check in at the pub, drop off our stuff, then explore Gladstone," Peter said.

"Check into a pub? Isn't that like a bar?"

He grinned. "Well, only a bit like a bar. They sell beer, cider, and some hard liquor. The term 'Pub' is short for 'Public house.' To get a license to sell alcohol, they need to rent rooms at a reasonable rate."

"That's kind of cool, but staying in a drinking house still sounds weird. Can't we stay at a normal motel?"

"Sally says it's a cultural experience we shouldn't miss. Let's at least look at it."

It occurred to me I had turned twenty-one after leaving the United States. I'd never been able to order a drink in a bar. "You know, I've never ordered a legal drink out. I wasn't old enough when we left the States."

Peter grinned and squeezed my hand. "Well, Australians will think you're really behind in development; the legal age here is eighteen.

Want to have a legal drink at our pub tonight?"

"Sure. I'm trying to be open to new experiences."

We stopped in front of a white building with a wide veranda with tables filled with loud people. The sign above the door said, *Queens Hotel*. The two of us walked up the steps, crossed the veranda, and walked into the main serving room. It was crowded and loud, and it smelled of beer. I tried to keep an open mind about spending the night. I waited for Peter to find out about our room. He came back with a room key.

We went up a flight of stairs and down a hall. Our room was last on the right. It was a nice room. Plain but clean and nice. The bed had an old-fashioned quilt, and the window had a view of the street with all the vendors. It was a bit noisy, but it would do.

"Are we still planning on visiting Little India for dinner?" I was getting hungry.

"Do you want to?" Peter asked.

"I think so. I'd still want to go out and see the town, and dinner out would be a good part of it."

"Better than eating here?" he asked.

"Yeah. The smell and the noise downstairs are a bit hard to take."

"Okay, let's explore."

On the way into the port, we had a good look at the commercial port where the international trade ships docked and the ferry station. But there was a lot more to Gladstone, and we only had an afternoon and an evening to explore. The region had extensive agricultural fields westward from the coast and another section with a complex of industrial factories. Australia had become a major player in the production of solar panels and batteries.

I wasn't interested in seeing agricultural fields or factories, but I was interested in seeing some of the network of residential communities. When a major storm threatened, the port evacuated, and workers went home and stayed safe on inland, non-vulnerable land. Each residential complex had shops, schools, parks, and local entertainment. We were heading to a residential community with the name "Little India."

I doubted the city planners intended towns to take on ethnic flavors, but people wanted to live near people they identified with, and there was a large enough industry and agricultural base to support several distinctively different towns.

We stepped off the tram, and I felt like we were in another country. In front of us, a woman was wearing a beautiful flowing silk dress.

"It's called a saree," Peter said.

"Wow," I said. "She's beautiful, and the dress is stunning."

There were food stands that smelled amazing and folks talking in a language I didn't understand. The name "Little India" seemed appropriate.

"Why do you think Australia has so many Indian immigrants?" I asked.

Peter looked at me, saying nothing, but his eyes were watery. Eventually, he said, "You know why."

I remembered why and felt like an idiot.

At the peak of climate collapse, repeated droughts led to widespread famine in India. International relief efforts were exhausted as countries coped with their own floods, droughts, and fires. Mass graves became a part of the Indian landscape as the lack of food, clean water, and medicine caused millions of deaths.

Of course, Australia had to accept climate refugees.

Australia escaped climate collapse without a massive death toll. They were under considerable pressure to accept refugees, and Indians willing to work on food plantations were given priority relocation. Obviously, many of these refugees ended up working in the agricultural fields surrounding Gladstone.

I looked around and started getting excited. Mom made some Indian dishes, but I'd never been to an actual Indian restaurant. "I bet the food is going to be great"

We found a restaurant that looked small and intimate and not too expensive. I had a wonderful lentil dish called dal makhani. Peter had a vegetable dish. We had fun sharing and tasting all the side dishes.

Over dinner, we talked about the trams that transported workers to residential, elevated towns further inland, which meant that after a flooding event, people had dry homes to return to.

By the time we got back to the pub, all I wanted to do was go to sleep, but I was a good sport and went in for a cider to keep Peter company. It wasn't bad at all.

And I was looking forward to eating our lamingtons in the morning.

Chapter 18~ Samantha~Back to Reality

Visiting Gladstone had been like a mental holiday, but I couldn't avoid my avatar issue forever. The local octopuses had fled in terror at the sight of S.A.M. I needed to figure out how to regain their trust and our progress.

Dr. Snyder waited for us as our ferry pulled into the harbor. The crew gathered the supplies from the boat and loaded them onto his cart. Together, we walked the supplies to the lab room. He smiled ear-to-ear when he opened the freezer box, revealing ample amounts of dry ice and his still-frozen biological reagents.

Peter and I exchanged a nod. Then Peter asked, "How often have you had to dump thawed reagents?"

Dr. Kelly said, "Only twice. Two years ago, I started sending staff to Gladstone to repack dry ice like you did. It's a bit of a pain, but it solves the problem."

I asked, "Why don't they use enough dry ice to last the full trip?"

He shook his head and shrugged. But then he offered some thoughts.

"I think it's a judgment call. The company gets charged by the box size, and they put as much dry ice into the container as will fit. It's enough ice for the trip from Melbourne to Heron if there are no delays, like a train missing the connection in Sydney or Brisbane."

Peter asked, "How often are there delays?"

Dr. Kelly said, "Not often, and they use enough ice, so the supplies say frozen, even with a missed connection. That means 95 percent of the time, everything is fine. They would rather replace lost shipments in the rare case they thaw than pay the increased shipping costs."

I said, "I can see why you sent someone. The delay in waiting for replacements would be maddening."

Dr. Kelly nodded in agreement.

Peter put his arm around my waist and said, "Well, we had a good time in Gladstone. Thanks for sending us."

"Glad you enjoyed the outing." He looked at the clock and said, "You have a couple of hours before our meeting. Why don't you relax? I'm looking forward to hearing about your progress on the communication project. I hear the use of the avatar had an interesting response."

I felt a warm flush on my face, imagining the jokes and kidding I would face at the meeting.

***

Outside the research lab, we walked on a narrow path through the tropical shrubs to our cabin. In some ways, Heron Island was so like Coastal Eleven that I often forgot I wasn't home. But the muttonbird songs reminded me to watch my step. They nest on the ground in burrows; I stepped into a hole a few weeks ago and landed in the mud. We don't have anything like muttonbirds back home.

Peter opened the door to our cabin, stepped inside, and turned the lights and ceiling fan on. I tossed my bag onto the bed and took my shoes off. It was nice to be back on the island.

I flopped into our hammock chair in the corner. It hung in the corner from a rafter, and I loved the simplicity and the relaxing motion. I needed to negotiate for one at home.

"Peter, can we brainstorm a bit before our meeting? Dr. Snyder is expecting an update on the octopus communication project, and I'm at a loss for what to say."

He came behind me and massaged my shoulders. "Samantha, I haven't been as involved with your project as I usually am back home. They have me multitasking to a ridiculous degree. So, I'm a bit lost. I've heard you talk about your octopus problem. What happened on the last dive?"

"I tried the avatar out with a group at station one: a Brother and a few Younglings—or whatever they call them here. I tried to have S.A.M. give a greeting. The group released a cloud of black ink and jetted away."

Peter looked like he was trying hard not to laugh. "I'm guessing it wasn't the reaction you were hoping for. Are you going to try it again?"

"That's the question. Should I? And I'm nervous that I might have scared them away for good."

Peter turned, looked out the window toward the blue ocean, and squeezed my shoulder. "No way, Samantha. They'll be back. You know they will."

"I hope so. But then what? Should I try the avatar again?"

I waited for an answer. Peter was quiet, still looking out the window. "Peter?"

"Samantha, when we used the avatar back in Georgia, Charlie and Archimedes showed signs of shock and discomfort, but they trusted us and weren't scared. Were you expecting the same response here?"

"I guess so," I said.

"You know, I've only been out on this reef with you a few times, but I think the problem is that the blue octopus reminds us so much of our friends back home that we forget they have limited experience with humans. You prepared Charlie and Archimedes before showing them the avatar."

"You think I jumped the gun here?"

He said, "I think you did. Charlie and the Elders were already in awe of what humans can do. To the Nest, the avatar was just another example of our technology. After the initial shock, they just rolled with it."

I nodded. "My mistake was forgetting the Australian octopuses don't know us and have no experience with *any* technology."

"You've got your answer. In our meeting with Dr. Snyder, we need to propose backing up and taking a slower approach."

"Peter, I agree. If I get the opportunity to try again, I want to start like we did with Charlie–using color sequences and moving coral. But I scared them off. What if they don't come back?"

He laughed. "They'll be back. Think about it. What would Charlie have done if you spooked him early on?"

"He would have moved away and watched from a distance."

Peter nodded. "He'd be dying of curiosity. I doubt he could stay away. I think *this* group will watch from a distance for a while. They will approach again. You know Charlie would have."

"We're diving again on Friday. Can you come with us?"

He said, "Yes, I'm caught up enough with preparing material for Mark and Jerry to use. I would enjoy a dive. I hate spending so much time preparing materials for Mark to deliver to the Georgia Nest. I'd like to be more involved here."

I said, "Great. You just gave me an idea. Mark meets with Charlie and Runt several times weekly for the lessons you prepare. Do you think he could organize a long-distance chat with Charlie, one where we could ask for advice?"

A wide grin spread across Peter's face. "That's a great idea. Who would be better to ask? Learner was able to break the communication barrier with the Cuban octopuses. Ask Mark to have Learner join the meeting. We need her insight."

I nodded. "I've wanted to try a long-distance meeting. This gives us a nice reason to try the equipment out."

I said, "We'll use the next dive to see how bad they're spooked. Let's just look and see if any octopuses are in the area. Then we can talk with

Mark and see when he can set a meeting up."

"I think you've decided what to discuss in today's team meeting. Feeling better?" he asked.

I nodded. "Yes, I do. I'm going to send an email to Mark and Jerry right now. They should see it when they wake up."

Peter looked at his watch and nodded. "It's 4:00 a.m. in Georgia. I wonder how quickly they'll be able to organize a meeting."

"Me too."

Chapter 19~ Samantha ~ Gone!

Heron Reef, Australia

As I feared, the dive was a bust—not an octopus in sight. We've been out to the reef twice since then, but still no octopuses. It took Mark a week to arrange the meeting, and I was impressed that he could get everything together quickly. I just hoped it would help. Even if it didn't, today would be an exciting event: the first telecommunication with octopuses between Australia and the United States.

We gathered in the conference room, watching a video feed from the reef webcam in the Coastal Eleven lagoon. On Coastal Eleven, this part of the lagoon was a favorite location of mine. Six years ago, I started walking the reef on my own and met Charlie for the first time. I was a teenager. You could say we grew up together. Now, Charlie was an Elder in every sense; he was a respected leader and also one of the oldest members of the Nest. No one knew how long this new race of intelligent octopuses lived, but I would be very sad when my friend died.

Behind us, the Heron research team was sitting on folding chairs, far enough back not to disturb Peter and me but close enough to see the monitor and hear the conversation. We were expecting Mark, the lead biologist, and my brother, Jerry. We hoped Charlie, Runt, and Learner would come and expected other Elders from the Nest would be watching. Although they would stay back, and we might not see them.

"Here they come," Peter said, pointing to the divers gliding down from the boat.

As they reached the sand, Jerry set up his tripod and camera. The camera was a sophisticated device that allowed us to see the action and feed the digital information to the translation computer. Mark rolled two mats onto the sand, connecting each to a control tablet or computer.

I would be controlling the tablet that would host my avatar, S.A.M., and regardless of the outcome, I was excited to take part in the meeting remotely.

Mark would operate the second mat, an older mat that displayed simple color sequences for communication. We all decided he would use the older technology because running two avatars would be confusing. I watched as I turned both displays on. I tapped Peter on the shoulder. It was time for us to get ready; we were not passive observers for this meeting.

I watched Charlie, Runt, and Learner drift into view, settling onto the sand near the mats. Behind them, a school of parrot fish grazed on rock rubble, ignoring the humans and octopuses nearby. The brightly colored parrot fish had few predators and fearlessly migrated around the reef.

Mark typed on his tablet, and we watched the color sequence move across his mat.

Thirty seconds later, the computer voice came through the speaker below the monitor. "Samantha will be using the avatar to take part in the meeting. Because she is in Australia, there will be a time delay. Please be patient."

I started typing my opening message using the keyboard. I hit send and watched, waiting for the avatar to respond. When S.A.M. began moving, I heard a sigh of relief from the team members behind us. Everyone had been holding their breath.

I was startled when *my* voice came from the speaker, "Charlie, Learner, and Runt, it is so good to see you. Thank you for agreeing to meet."

Peter started to laugh and punched me lightly on my arm. "The techs are mimicking your voice. That's funny."

"Yeah, very funny."

Peter pulled his chair close to the desk and whispered, "Every time I see the translation equipment in action, I'm amazed. I wish I could understand the details of how it works."

I nodded. "It's amazing. I gave up trying to understand the technology. As long as I can use it and it works, I'm satisfied."

"Me too, I guess," he said.

"Still, I get asked lots of questions about the technology during the public talks Dr. Kelly has me giving. I do wish I understood more about how the system works."

"I'm glad he has you doing them, not me," Peter said.

"I wonder why Kelly has <u>me</u> doing the public outreach. You're the one with a public relations degree."

"I've watched you, and you're a natural."

"Thanks, I guess. I can't say I love doing them. I get so nervous."

He said, "The more you do, the easier it will get."

Then we stopped talking. Charlie had moved onto the sand. We watched his tentacles gracefully moving as he messaged, and a blue and green light sequence moved across his head and tentacles.

It seemed to take forever for the computer voice to deliver the translation. Then the male voice came through the speaker, *"How long have you been meeting with the blue octopus Nest?"*

I typed my reply and waited. Soon, the avatar was in motion.

The digital image was relatively flat. It had lost some of the amazing three-dimensional effects I had grown used to. Watching on a monitor was different from viewing the avatar close-up underwater.

S.A.M.'s tentacles moved. I watched in wonder as my virtual octopus placed virtual rock pieces onto the virtual sand. Even with the image somewhat flattened on the display, it was surreal.

"Ten high tides," I heard my voice come through the speaker. *"Long enough that I hoped I had their trust."*

Learner moved into the central position, and we watched her send the message, *"Do you have a translation program for the blue octopus?"*

I responded using the avatar, "No, we are in the early stage of that work."

Her response was immediate and emphatic, *"Then it was too early to use the avatar."*

I said, *"I know that now. Do you have any advice on how to fix this? What should we do now?"*

We watched Charlie and Learner exchange a flurry of tentacle motions and colors on our monitor. Eventually, the computer would provide a translation, but it would take some time. All we could do was wait.

Chapter~20~Advice From Home

Coastal Eleven, Georgia

Learner and I were early for our meeting. It was an hour before the high tide. A gentle breeze moved the surface of the water creating a sparkle effect on the sand and soft corals of the lagoon where they would meet with the team. A school of grunts and parrot fish moved through the area, providing relief to the stillness. The lagoon waters were quiet this morning.

Charlie moved onto the sand and arranged fragments as part of his message. *"Learner, they are coming here for advice on the use of the avatar and communicating with the blue octopus. You are to advise – not offer to go to Australia."*

Learner's colors darkened as she watched fish in the distance. Then, she answered, *"I have had enough travel, but don't know what to advise them."*

"Just be ready to answer questions. They asked for you because you broke through when their language specialists could not. Your accomplishment identified you as a valuable resource."

Learner's colors lightened, andshe responded with colors indicating unease, but also resolve. *"In Cuba, I observed the local octopuses and then tried to mimic the way they communicated. I don't know how to do this without being there."*

"This is not like the situation in Cuba, where we had to rescue Samantha, and time was limited. Humans can take as long as they need to reach a breakthrough with the Australian octopuses."

"I still have no idea how to advise them. Do you?" Learner asked, moving off the sand and settling with her tentacles wrapped around the base of a sea fan.

"I think they should stop using the avatar and go back to using color sequences on the display mat. It will be less threatening. The avatar can be introduced after they have some basic communication in place."

Learner signaled agreement and motioned toward the surface. A boat approached the reef crest. As it moved closer, the shadow of the boat crossed the sand. The team would join us any time now.

She messaged, *"I need to see the blue octopus interacting with each other. It is likely Samantha recorded interactions. Can we ask Mark to display them for us?"*

"I think that will be worthwhile. But remember, you won't be able to try messaging like you did in Cuba. You won't be able to see what works."

Learner signaled that she understood and added, *"I can see why Samantha wants to have the avatar to use. If I could operate an avatar through Samantha, it would allow us to test messages. That will have to wait."*

"At least for now, we will identify patterns in movements and color sequences. It is how I would start if I were on the reef."

A disturbance at the surface interrupted our exchange, and we watched as two divers made their way down to us. We moved to the patch of sand and waited while Jerry set the cameras in place, Mark initiated the display mat, and S.A.M., the avatar, came into view.

I examined S.A.M. and tried to imagine what I would have thought if Samantha had caused him to appear at our first meeting or even during one of the early meetings when we were first working on a shared vocabulary. *Would I have dropped black ink and jetted away? I'd like to think I am braver than that, but I'm not sure.*

95

Chapter 21 ~Samantha~ Starting Over

It felt like I had rewound the past six weeks. Dr. Snyder sent a larger team now that our goal had shifted to making observations and recording behavior rather than attempting contact. Three teams of two divers were positioned twenty meters apart on the reef. Each team had a diver working a camera and a second diver with a display mat and a camera. The diver display mat had a pre-programmed greeting.

There were no octopuses on-site. This was disappointing but not unexpected. Dr. Snyder wanted us to observe and record the activity of fish and invertebrates like crabs and other invertebrates while we waited, hoping that one or more of the colony members would be curious and show up. I hoped that they had not been so spooked that they migrated away from this area. Charlie recommended we observe the area for at least a few weeks before trying another part of the reef. He thought they would hide for a while but eventually approach again.

Part of me was frustrated by the lack of progress. It was difficult to keep my type A personality in check. But part of me enjoyed being on this magnificent reef and observing. Dr. Snyder assured us that observations and video recordings were valuable documentation of Heron Reef, a kind of timestamp of conditions. And this was the Great Barrier Reef. Being on any reef was, in my book, a privilege. Being on this reef was like winning the lottery.

Before me, a carpet of colors spanned as far as I could see. At five meters, the reds had disappeared, and some of the oranges had also dimmed, but the shades of green, purple, blue, and yellow created a dazzling coral mosaic. There was an impressive diversity of coral here, and all of it seemed to be thriving. Heron Island was on the southern end of the reef, and while global warming had increased the ocean temperature, we were still in a favorable range for coral health.

I know it's confusing. In the southern hemisphere, the North is warmer, and the South is cooler. So, being on the reef's south end, we see fewer issues with bleaching and other warming effects.

A juvenile lionfish spread his spines like a fan in the water before me. It moved with a slow elegance as if it were dancing on a stage. Lionfish spines had a neurotoxin similar to cobra venom. They were rather brazen about swimming out in the open, alone and unprotected. Back home, they were invasive and had no natural predators. They were a disruptive force before scientists developed marine drones to target lionfish. They weren't eliminated, but population numbers were kept low.

Seeing this fellow brought a smile to my face. The lionfish on this reef integrated into the ecosystem, adding stability and beauty. Yes, I would enjoy being part of an observation team until the octopuses decided to approach us again, but I hoped that wouldn't be too far in the future.

Peter waved to me, and I moved in his direction. Once we were in range, his voice came through to my earpiece.

"I saw one. They're still here," he said.

"That's a relief. Did he approach?" I asked.

"No, and I wanted to be as non-threatening as I could, so I only recorded him from a distance. But I think he's watching us."

I gave Peter a thumbs-up. "Glad he's here. I'm not even going to unroll the mat. For now, let's just keep making general observations. Let them get used to our presence again."

He nodded. "I can't believe the number of sea cucumber species here."

He was right. In the last few days, I had counted and photographed over twenty different species of sea cucumbers. Sea cucumbers were echinoderms that took in small rocks and sand from the sea floor, scraped algae and nutrients off the sand grains, and expelled them. Many people thought they were plants, but if you watched long enough, you saw that they move, just slowly. We had them in the Atlantic, but not in the rainbow of colors we were seeing here.

I said, "The starfish are also incredible. It's like an explosion of species diversity here. Why settle for one or two species of something when you can have twenty?"

As we moved along the reef wall, a school of parrot fish swam between us, sweeping from above and disappearing below a ledge. I glanced at my pressure gauge. I had enough air for at least fifteen or twenty minutes. Peter had seen one of the blue octopuses, and I wished he would show up again. I'd like to know if he was the one I had been working with, trying to initiate communication.

At first, all octopuses looked alike, but I'd been interacting with octopuses long enough that the subtle differences had become obvious. I felt certain I would recognize the fellow I scared. I still felt terrible about causing him so much distress.

In the distance, I noticed one team working their way up the anchor line. I double-checked my gauge. I still had plenty of air.

"Peter, how are you on air?" I asked.

"I'm fine. I should be okay for another ten minutes of bottom time. Do you need to head back?"

"No, but I see divers returning to the boat. I wonder if something's wrong."

Peter said, "Let's move closer to the anchor line. But, Jim would have banged on the hull if he needed us back."

"We do use our air slower than most of the Australians, but I'm a bit cold and wouldn't mind going back to the boat with a bit of air left in the tank."

We started toward the anchor line when I saw the outline of a bronze whaler on the other side of the boat. We didn't see bronze whalers in Georgia, or at least I'd never seen one. These were fat sharks and intimidating to look at, not like the sleek reef sharks we saw all the time back home. To be honest, even the small reef sharks gave me an adrenaline rush. Ever since the night I ended up swimming in from a reef crest at night, I'd had a low tolerance for being in the water with sharks. It was irrational. This is their home! Even in my night swim, they didn't bother me. However, that night, whenever I saw a fin close, I swam even harder toward shore. Sometimes, it felt like the shark was so close I could reach out and touch it.

I was getting used to seeing bronze whalers, and I tried not to over-react. The Australians ignored them, saying they weren't aggressive sharks. The problem was they looked a lot like the bull sharks back home—large, fat-looking sharks that were high on the aggression scale. I felt my heart rate increase while I tried to stay calm.

Peter saw the shark almost as soon as I did. He had his camera out and was taking a video. He put the camera away after a few minutes. He knew these guys made me uneasy.

"I think we've made enough observations for today. Let's head up," he said.

"Thanks. I know I'm a wimp, but right now, I think I'd rather be in the boat rather than down here."

Together, we went up the anchor line, keeping an eye on our very large friend.

Chapter 22 ~ Blue Encounter

The visitors came back. This time there were more of them in their group, and they spread out in pairs. I brought the news to the Elder Counsel. They asked me to return and make observations. They assigned three Brothers to travel with me.

"Why are you assigning Brothers to come with me?" I asked.

"We don't want you alone. We don't want any Brothers or Elders alone when these strange creatures are on the reef."

"Should we approach them?"

"Not yet. Just observe from a distance. Report back what they are doing."

That was how I found myself with three Brothers, watching two of the visitors at the reef wall. The four of us stayed out of sight as we watched the strange beings.

I felt my ridges pulsing and tried to calm my movements. And soon, I felt relief since they seemed to be harmless. They were in pairs, observing fish, coral, and other parts of the reef. Each pair settled into an area rich with coral and other life. Once they were in place, they remained still. It seemed like they were trying to fix the life before them into memory. No fish or any life were eaten or taken captive. *Were my memories of the ghost Brother just imagination, the result of fear of the unknown?*

I thought I recognized one visitor. We had interacted in the past. She had brought me treats. But she was also the one who frightened me, who had a magic Brother. *Was she dangerous? I was still fearful but now questioned my own memories.* We stayed with the pair until they rose to the surface and disappeared. The other visitors, two at a time, traveled to the same spot on the reef wall, rose to the surface, and also disappeared. Then, we watched a shadow on the surface move away from the reef wall. The visitors were gone, and a tension left me. When I looked at my Brothers, I could see their colors had become light again. They, too, were relieved the strange visitors were gone.

"*Should we return to the Elder Counsel and report?*" a Brother asked.

"*Yes,*" I said and led my group down the wall and into a crevice opening to our Nest.

After making our report, we waited. It was uncomfortable. I wanted to be part of the discussion and decision. But I was not an Elder, so we waited. The Brothers with me seemed content to just wait, but I was not. They had not seen the captive Brother. To them, the visitors seemed harmless. Maybe they were.

An Elder approached, and I presented my greeting. He responded with an acknowledgment and then addressed our group.

"*You were not alone in seeing the visitors. Other Brothers messaged the visitors are at the reef in greater numbers now, and they seem to follow behavior that we have seen before,*" he said.

"*I am pleased other groups confirm our observation,*" I replied.

The Elders' colors darkened, and he moved closer for his next message. "*The Council wants observation on the visitors when they are aware of our presence. They want to see if the visitors will try to send a message.*"

I felt my ridges pulse, and a coldness flowed over me. What he said made sense, but I did not wish to approach these creatures. A memory of the captive Brother, the ghost, haunted me. *Did I have to go back? Did I have to confront them?* My distress must have been clear. The Elder reached for me reassuringly.

He said, "*We are asking all groups to send a message to the Nest as soon as the visitors return. The Council wants an Elder to be present. If you do not wish to be present at the interaction, we will understand.*"

"No, I will go. It is true I am uneasy with them. But I am more curious. I want to go."

"*We are pleased. The Counsel feels that if you are willing, you should be the contact since they have met with you already.*"

I could see the logic in the request and signaled my acceptance.

He messaged, "*You will not be alone. I am coming, and others from the Council as well.*"

It took another two light periods before the visitors returned. Word reached the Nest as soon as they entered the water. We hurried to the location, knowing these visitors did not remain underwater for long.

Chapter 23 ~ Samantha ~ Contact

Blue approached us on our sixth observational visit. Peter and I were documenting grouper under ledges of the reef wall when he came into view and settled on the sand before us. As we watched, he arranged fragments of coral into a pattern. Charlie predicted they would watch for a while, then approach us. *This was it.* I felt my heart race and glanced at Peter, who shifted the camera and was recording Blue.

It was early in our dive, and I wondered if perhaps he had been waiting for us. Charlie cautioned me to go slow. But Blue obviously wanted to make contact, so I unrolled the mat and gave the pre-programmed greeting. I noticed we had company, an assemblage of octopuses watched from staghorn coral at the base of the reef wall.

Were they watching us or Blue? He was looking at us, but he kept looking back at his companions. I knew enough about octopus mannerisms to tell he was nervous. His colors drifted between purple and dark blue, making him appear brooding. His ridges pulsed almost in a spasm. He was clearly agitated. When he looked at his companions, I was left with the impression that he was only meeting with us because they were compelling him too. That made me feel awkward. Not only had I frightened him, but now, I was responsible for placing him in an uncomfortable situation.

But I was grateful that for whatever reason, he was here. It felt like he was giving me a second chance. I reached into my bag, retrieved a crab, and placed it on the sand. It wasn't on my agenda, but I was certain we had a history. I had given him treats in the past. Hopefully, offering this treat would remind him of our prior interactions before I tried the avatar—a time before Blue became fearful of the avatar.

He considered the offering and glanced once more at his companions. They looked non-committal. He reached and accepted the treat, his colors drifting to light blue and his ridges slowed, the erratic movements becoming a smooth rhythmic and gentle pulse. While Blue gracefully dismembered and devoured the crab.

I sent a one-word message to the display, "Crab".

He looked at the mat, giving no sign of interest. I removed a second crab from my bag and repeated the message, "Crab."

This time, Blue seemed interested. He turned to the observers and displayed a rapid sequence of color changes.

"Peter, are you getting this?" I asked.

"I am," he said. "I'm on it. Concentrate on what you are doing."

I gave Peter a thumbs-up and continued.

Blue was unnaturally still, but his colors were light, showing no sign of agitation or fear. His large eyes fixed on the crab in front of us. Then he moved a tentacle touching the crab between us and presenting a color sequence that danced across his head and tentacles. His color sequence was different from the one I had used. *Did he understand what I was doing? That I was trying to build a dictionary?* I felt a wave of excitement. Our work began.

I pointed at the staghorn coral bringing my finger within a centimeter but not touching the sensitive polyps.

"Staghorn coral," I messaged with a color sequence on the mat.

Blue looked at the mat then at me and back at the octopuses behind us. They were watching us intently. He placed a tentacle near the staghorn and a color sequence moved across his head and tentacles.

The school of parrot fish was close by. I took a chance and moved to point to one of them. Returning to the mat I signaled, "Parrotfish."

Blue followed my lead, pointing to the fish and initiating a sequence. We continued with my name game until Peter's voice in my ear informed me we needed to return to the boat, the air in his tank was below the safety margin. I checked my gauge and to my horror saw that I was almost out of air. I had one thing I wanted to try before ending the session.

I told Peter to give me a minute, and I pointed to the staghorn coral and repeated my color sequence. I wanted to know, would Blue be consistent in what he used to respond[JB1] ? I couldn't remember so as I watched him respond, I didn't have an answer to that question. But Peter had been recording and the computer linguists would run their analysis as soon as we uploaded the data. So, we would know soon enough. That answer would tell us if Blue understood I was trying to exchange vocabulary with his kind, and if he was responding with names for the organisms.

Just for the heck of it, I messaged, "Goodbye," before detaching my phone from the mat, rolling it up, and following Peter back to the anchor line. I noticed that he too sent a final color sequence.

Had we made progress? Well, yes, they were no longer hiding from us. But how much progress had we made? I was surprisingly optimistic.

We would send our video to the States, and ask Mark to show it to Charlie and Learner. I wanted to hear their views on our progress and suggestions for the next step.

[JB1]I stumbled over the wording here. Is there a less wordy way to say this?

Chapter 24 ~Blue~ Questions and Answers

With the creatures spending more time on the reef, in greater numbers, we had time to observe them from a distance. I'd always been prone to worry and nerves, and when the Council instructed me to approach the visitors again, it was hard not to feel like I was being offered as a sacrifice. But I agreed that these creatures were simply watching fish and other life; they seemed harmless. So, I was nervous but not terrified. For me, that was good.

Still, my tentacles were dark, almost black, and my ridges stiffened and twitched as I approached the creatures. I had to get my nerves under control, so I retreated into a tangle of branch coral and worked to calm myself.

I focused my attention on a coral polyp extended into the water feeding. The polyps moved in flowing, graceful motion. Pushing all other thoughts away and concentrating on the polyp worked. My color shifted to a lighter shade of blue, and my ridges no longer felt like they would explode. I glanced back at the Elders, who had gathered a short distance from where I worked through my fears. Typically, their presence would make me nervous, but today, their presence was a comfort.

The Council members saw me looking toward them. One member signaled a question, *"Are you okay?"*

I signaled, *"If I say no, will you send someone else?"*

I watched as the group exchanged a flurry of colors between each other. *They thought I was kidding, and they were laughing at my joke. That was what I got—laughter! Their laughter made me angry, and that was good. Anger made it easier to ignore the* [JB1]

If something happened to me, they would try to help. And my Brothers would know my fate if I was captured or killed. The Elders on the Counsel told me they were *honoring me* when they assigned this task. *Why couldn't they honor someone with an adventurous spirit? But no, they picked me.*

It was time. I needed to do the job to show my Elders could count on me. I moved out from the safety of the coral forest and toward the creature. There was a familiarity to this one. I was sure I had seen it before. I kept my distance but moved to where I knew it would see me.

At first, the creature ignored me. I moved closer, and it offered food. *Should I take it?* The Elders motioned for me to accept the gift. I strove to maintain my calm, approached, and accepted the food. The Elders were motioning that I needed to eat the gift. I had to make myself eat while watching for any sign of aggression, but the creature seemed friendly. At least, I could not detect any aggression.

The creature spread an object on the sand between us. The object covered the sand, and as I watched, lights flashed over the sand. I had seen this before. And, at least this time, there was no sign of a captive Brother.

The creature pointed to the colors on the object and to a crab they offered. Were they naming the crab? If so, they had the sequence of colors wrong. *"Young crab."*

I ate the crab and waited.

The large creature hovered over the sand, watching and unmoving. A stream of bubbles rose from the front of its face giving evidence that like dolphins, this was an air breather.

This creature was about the size of a small dolphin but slow-moving.

While I waited, it seemed to point to the finger coral, and another sequence of colors moved across the sand. My excitement banished fear. These were intelligent beings, and their intent was communication.

I touched the finger coral and provided the color sequence and tentacle motion we used to identify this coral. *Do they understand me? How can I tell if they understand me?*

I moved to a sponge, pointed to it, and gave the name. *"Sponge."* Then I pointed to the creature, then to the sponge, then to the creature again.

The creature pointed to the sponge, and my color sequence flashed across the sand. It appeared to accept the name I provided. *This creature was trying to use our language.* I glanced back at the Elders and watched their excited movements and colors. They saw it, and their bright colors and rapid tentacle motions indicated that they, too, recognized the attempt at communication.

I tried to visualize the octopus I had seen in the device on the sand. Did they have an octopus captive? I was no longer sure. *What had I seen?*

I had to try something to see if my thoughts about communication had strength. I gave the same sequence and motions I used for *"Crab"* again and waited. The creature gave no response. I messaged again, this time pointing to them. After a short period of stillness, the creature produced another crab and offered the treat to me. I was more confident now. The creature had used light sequences to name the crab and the coral. This was an attempt at communication.

I signaled my thanks and ate the crab. The creature removed the object that displayed colors from the sand. I watched this strange school of creatures travel across the reef floor, and then they rose as a group and disappeared from the water as they entered the unknown region beyond. I rejoined the Council members, waiting with growing signs of impatience. As I approached, my mentor jetted over and met me.

"We thank you for contacting these creatures," he said. *"You did very*

well."

"*They are not as frightening as I thought. Why did they leave?*" I asked.

"*They are air breathers and can't stay long when they visit,*" he said.

I could no longer think about these creatures and the meaning of our encounter. A weariness overtook me. I needed rest.

"*The encounter was intense. May I rest now?*" I asked.

"*Rest. We understand.*" He said.

Excusing myself, I sought the comfort of solitude.

[JB1]We're missing part of this sentence.

Chapter 25 ~ Samantha ~News From Home

Shelter From The Storm

We returned to the lab and uploaded the video and computer data. The Georgia Tech crew would start building a database of color sequences and movements, which would be the start of a new "dictionary."

I wanted to talk with Dr. Kelly, but it was two a.m., so I sent a text message and was surprised when my phone rang and I saw he was on the line.

"Why are you awake?" I asked.

"I'm working evacuation again. No rest for the weary," Dr. Kelly said.

That made me stop in my tracks. On Heron Island, there were no news broadcasts from the United States. Everyone focused on the reef and local news. It was the wrong season here for major storms, and I forgot this was hurricane season back home. Of course, hurricane seas stretched from May to December now, more than half the year. But this was September, and the storms could be fierce.

"Has Coastal Eleven been evacuated?" I asked.

"Yes, they are at the shelter now. Your Mom, Mark, and Jerry are all fine."

I felt guilty that I hadn't been watching the news, but these days, the news rarely covered hurricane evacuations unless there were many casualties or intense property damage. The authorities had gotten good at getting people off vulnerable lands and not building where the damage would be intense. So, we were making progress. Still, I remembered spending the night in the shelter for Hurricane Gigi back in 2044. I had been insanely worried about Charlie and the Nest back then.

"Did you get a warning to the Nest to move to deep water?"

"We did. You will be impressed. We built the octopus shelter and had a hurricane warning system in place. The Elders moved everyone to the site before we even evacuated the island."

"That's great," I said.

I had approved the plans for the octopus shelter but hadn't been at Coastal Eleven when they installed the multipurpose structure. Over 100 octopuses were living on the Coastal Eleven reef. They were usually spread over a three-kilometer span of reef, and it was rare to find them in high density at any location. In 2044, we had a category six hurricane moving into the area and warned the Nest that the storm would be fierce. They dispersed into deep water and hunkered down. It was dangerous for them because that was the area where large sharks dominated. So, we put the Georgia Tech folks in charge of designing a better solution for a storm shelter.

They devised a multipurpose low-lying dome anchored on the sea floor, butting up against the reef edge. It kind of looked like a science fiction rendering of a moon base. It had five entrances that were small enough to keep large predators out. The engineers worked hard to design vents to manage the storm waves and surging currents to keep the water flowing and not stagnant while protecting the octopuses from being tossed around.

Charlie and Archimedes were both impressed with the structure. They had a crew of Brothers assigned to maintenance, keeping fouling organisms from reducing water flow. A bigger worry was food in the aftermath of a storm, but I was glad to hear they were safe for now. I knew Dr. Kelly would handle food deliveries if the octopuses needed them.

"How bad of a storm are we looking at?" I asked.

"This one is a category five. We are taking all precautions," he said. "We'll be fine. I hope they won't need supplemental food this time, but we are ready with supplies if they need help."

"Sounds like you have your hands full. We can discuss our contact with the blue octopus group after the storm if you like."

"Not on your life! I'm busy but dying of curiosity. Give me an update."

"We followed Charlie and Learner's advice, backing off and making our presence known while making generic observations on the reef. We worked in teams of two divers, keeping six divers on the reef for a forty-five-minute dive each day. On the sixth dive, we had a visit from Blue. At least, I think it was the octopus I'd interacted with before. I think the Elders sent him as some kind of envoy.

"Many older octopuses were watching us. I'm assuming they are the equivalent of an Elder Council. Blue seemed skittish at first but relaxed once we interacted with the display mat and shared color sequences. I think Learner's idea of sharing the names of local animals was excellent. We will continue with this focus, hopefully building a dictionary and trust."

He said, "The Georgia Tech folks have been hounding me for updates on your work. When they wake up in the morning and open your message and files, they will be pleased to have something exciting to work on. I'm sure they will get right on it, but I doubt you will have an update to the translation software before you go out again."

"I'd also like Charlie and Learner to see the videos, they might have insights even before translations are available."

"Good idea. We're working on something you will be interested in."

"What?"

"We've wanted the Nest to have something better than just a call button for some time now. So, when we installed the permanent octopus shelters, we installed a high-tech communication station based on the satellite phones with translation software."

"Not to be a downer, but don't you need to relay the signal from the surface?"

"The shelter is at sixty meters. The engineers had fun working it out, but they are planning a tethered antenna station."

"That would be so awesome."

"Well, they are working on it, but it might be a while."

"I hope it won't be too long. We want to build on momentum. So, we'll send the computer files after each dive for a while. They can go to the computer crew for analysis, but they can also go to Mark so he can share them with Charlie and Learner."

"That sounds like a good plan. I'll tell the engineers that you're very excited about the communication station. Samantha, I'm going to get some sleep. I'll talk to you after the storm passes."

That brought me back to reality. "Stay safe," I said and hung up.

Chapter 26 ~ Blue~Language Lessons

We have exchanged names for dozens of fish and coral. They did not seem dangerous, but I was curious why they wanted to learn our names for things. The Council was intrigued, and I shared their curiosity. We used color sequences, tentacle motions, and positioning of rock rubble to communicate information to each other. This practice was helpful for hunting, assigning tasks, and sharing plans and information. We found no fish or life on the reef communicating with color sequences. There was talk that dolphins and whales might share information through the vibrations we felt in the water.

These strangers were using colors! They did not have tentacles, so they could not use motion to communicate. I saw the one who visits with me position coral rubble. They were trying to communicate. *What are they trying to tell us?*

The Council's interest remained high, but after a heated meeting, they had only one Elder observe rather than the group. They feared they were intimidating the visiting creatures. It was true they intimidated me, so I am happy that only my mentor now observed. He was with me today while I waited for the creatures to arrive.

"These creatures learn easily. I only need to give the name for a fish once, and they remember it," he said.

"We will run out of fish to name soon," I said. *"They are being methodical. I wonder if they will leave and not return when we no longer have fish and*

other life to name."

"When we teach our young to use messaging, we start with names. Then, when the youngsters are familiar with the idea of color sequences and motions, we move the lesson to include sequences for actions. When they are ready, they will move to messaging of actions. That is more difficult, and I will be interested to see how they approach the work."

"It will indeed be interesting. I wonder if I should try to start a lesson on action," I said.

His ridges pulsed, and his colors drifted from red to purple.

I waited for a response.

"You could try, but it will be a hard lesson. You might do better by waiting for their interest and responding to what they ask."

We both watched as the dark shadow moved across the sand. Soon, the tell-tale vibrations announced that the strangers were in the water and would approach me soon. My mentor retreated to his secure observation site. I did not need to wait long.

The creature rolled the color-making device onto the sand and triggered a sequence of colors they had always used when they arrived. This sequence never changed, and my mentor's words about the sequence of lessons returned to me. I wondered if it wasn't a name but an action.

Then, I realized that we started with a greeting when two or more octopuses came together. Was the creature's color sequence their greeting? I'd seen this sequence many times. Maybe this was their greeting for meeting with octopuses. We had many greetings, one for equals and one for a younger octopus to greet a mentor. It would not be strange if they had a specific greeting for meeting with strangers.

I responded with a greeting between equals. *Was this appropriate?* Who knew, but I used it anyway.

"I greet you and welcome you to our exchange," I messaged.

There was a long pause, and then the creature sent a sequence of colors back to the sand. This time, they repeated the sequence I had used. My mentor was correct. *These creatures learn quickly.*

I had another thought and signaled to my mentor that I wished him to approach. He seemed startled but did as I asked and moved forward to join me in front of the creature.

I carefully and formally greeted my mentor using the greeting of a youth to a respected Elder. It was excellent that we discussed expanding the lessons to include action. He understood what I was doing and responded with the greeting of a mentor to their young Brother.

Then we waited. The second creature moved toward the color device and waited. This creature was larger than the one I had been exchanging names with, and I wondered if this creature was older and a mentor. But when my visitor pointed to the larger creature and pointed to it, the color sequence was different. So not a mentor or a younger Brother. My mentor was correct. The lesson would be challenging. *What did the new color sequence signify?*

The visitor pointed to itself and gave a color sequence, then to the larger creature and gave the second sequence. The two sequences, like the two creatures, were distinct. B*ut what did the sequences mean?*

Then, the creature pointed to me and gave me the sequence my mentor had used to greet me. I don't think they understood the sequence was for a relationship. That might have been too difficult a concept for now.

I tried again, using the sequence "*Octopus*" and pointing first to my mentor and then to myself. Then I slowly pointed to each creature, one at a time, and waited. I didn't have to wait long.

"*Octopus,*" the creature messaged, pointing first toward me and then toward my mentor.

Once again, I pointed to each of the creatures.

The creature provided a color sequence, pointing first to the larger creature and then to itself.

I soon learned the sequence meant *human* and that our visitors were *humans*.

Chapter 27 ~Samantha ~ Life Issues

Heron Island, Australia

The dive wasn't hard or long, but I was exhausted and didn't know why. I was glad Peter reached for my tank and helped me into the boat. I sat on the bench, shivering, while he gathered our masks, snorkels, and fins, dipped them in fresh water, and gave everything a good rinse. The tanks would wait for their rinse until we were on shore.

"You look beat," he said and tossed me a heavy towel.

"Thanks," I said and wrapped the towel around my shoulders.

"Yeah, I feel beat. It wasn't that hard of a dive, but I feel like I need to sleep for a week."

"Maybe you're coming down with something," he said, placing his hand on my forehead.

"You feel cool, but that doesn't say much. You just got out of the water."

"I don't feel sick, just feel tired. I found the dive mentally exhausting. I didn't expect Blue to take charge like that."

"I didn't ether. He's smart and persistent," Peter said.

"He is. I think Blue is particularly intelligent and a natural leader."

Peter nodded. "It shouldn't come as a surprise that octopuses can have different personalities and abilities, just like people."

"They do. Back at the Nest, the Elders assign Younglings roles based on their characteristics. Charlie was an 'explorer' because of his adventurous spirit. I wonder if the Australian Council assigns jobs. If so, I wonder how Blue is classified."

Peter said, "I'm guessing they are grooming him for leadership."

"Sounds about right. He was timid when we began, and the Elders almost forced him to interact with us, but he was fine today. He seemed to be over his initial case of jitters."

The crystal-blue water was smooth, almost like glass. We moved through the channel without any boat bounce or roll, but I was feeling queasy. Something wasn't right.

"You know, I might be coming down with something. Either that or I'm getting seasick."

"You never get seasick," he said, feeling my forehead again. "I don't think you have a fever. But you should take it easy this afternoon. I'll let the lab team know you weren't feeling well. If you're on the brink of coming down with something, resting might help you fight it off."

"Good point. I don't want to get sick and miss the dives. If I don't show up, Blue might be disappointed. We aren't at the point where you could explain that I have a cold."

The boat pulled into the harbor, and I stood up to help with the ropes. *Why was Peter staring at me?* I had difficulty catching my breath, and the sun dimmed. Then I felt something hit my face, and everything went black.

When I could see again, I was in our cabin in bed. The room was crowded. Peter stood beside the bed, and Dr. Snyder stood by the window beside a woman wearing medical scrubs. *Did we have a doctor on the island?*

The clock said it was three p.m. The last I remembered it was before lunch, and I knew that because I'd been hungry. *How long was I out?*

I closed my eyes and tried to get everyone to disappear, but they were still there when I opened them.

"How do you feel?" Dr. Snyder asked.

"I'm okay. Did I pass out on the dock?"

The woman in scrubs stepped up to the bed. "Hi, Samantha, I'm Susan, part of the island medical team. Dr. Snyder asked me to check on you. And, yes, you passed out. Do you know where you are?"

"Heron Island, Australia," I said.

"That's good," she said.

I noticed a splint and bandage on my left wrist and asked, "What happened?"

"When you passed out on the dock, you smashed your wrist. I bandaged it. Can you tell me what you felt right before you passed out?"

"I remember trying to stand up and having problems. Nothing after that."

She nodded to Dr. Snyder and Peter.

Peter came over and took my unbandaged hand. "We're going to step outside. Susan wants a few words in private.

"Okay," I said.

They stepped out of our room, leaving us alone. She was a redhead and had a very light complexion. That must be rough on this island. She looked a bit older than me but still young.

"Samantha, your wrist will be fine; it's a minor sprain. But I'm concerned about you passing out. Have you ever passed out before today?"

"No, I don't think so," I said.

"Might you be pregnant?"

"I don't think so. I'm on birth control. We plan to wait until we both have our doctorates. But I guess it's possible."

She handed me a box with a pregnancy test. "Many things can cause a person to pass out, but since you are of childbearing age and in a relationship, we should check and see. No birth control is perfect."

"Do you want me to use this now?" I asked.

"Do you feel like you can get up?" she asked.

I nodded, moved my legs over the side of the bed, and tentatively put weight on my feet. "I'm okay."

She motioned to the toilet. "You might as well go ahead and take a test. It's important to know if you are pregnant. This test won't give a definitive result—it might be too early. But if it is positive, you'll need to make plans. And we won't need to send you for other medical tests. With you on the dive team, we need to know if you are at risk of passing out while underwater."

I nodded, took the package, and headed to the bathroom. I was still feeling a little lightheaded, but I wasn't sure if it was because I was sick or just nervous. *I'm too young to be a mother.*

Chapter 28 ~ Charlie~Hurricane Alice

Coastal Eleven, Georgia Barrier Island

The shelter's taste was not unique, but it was unusual. We had hunted in structures that tasted like this before. We now knew that these were abandoned ships by humans.

Metal was also the taste of safety. The humans were clever. The water moved, but not with the chaotic tumbling of the storm outside. I approached one opening and reached out with a tentacle. The movement threatened to pull me from the shelter. My other tentacles gripped the holdfasts, and I was glad the human engineers provided holdfasts so we could position observers at each entrance.

Archimedes waited for me at the central meeting chamber with Learner and Runt. The chamber was similar in size to our central chamber at the Nest. It could hold ten Elders. The walls were smooth and shiny. A few small parrot fish were swimming near the opening. We didn't eat parrot fish, so we ignored them. Other types of fish had migrated in seeking shelter, but I did not see them now.

As I approached, they moved aside and made room for me in front of the sand floor, a space planned and constructed by the humans for us.

"Tell us about the storm current," Archimedes said.

I smoothed the sand before me and selected three small rock fragments to show direction and location.

"I checked the east entrance. The water is moving very quickly. It is not safe to leave the shelter. I will check and report before the next rest cycle. "

Runt moved to the position across from me and tentatively messaged, *"There is enough food for the Younglings to last the storm. There is no need to leave the shelter to hunt."*

Mark and Jerry brought containers of food for the Younglings. Brothers and Elders were larger and could wait until the storm ended and we could hunt again.

I said, *"Let us hope the fish and crabs return after the storm."*

Archimedes, Runt, and Learner reacted to my statement with subdued colors.

Archimedes responded first, *"NOAA has installed baffles beyond the windward reef slope. It should lessen the impact of waves on the slope and reef flat."*

I tried to align Archimedes' comment with the water movement outside the entrance, where it took strength not to be carried away. If the water movement was this strong after crossing the baffles, what would it have been if the baffles were *not* in place?

Learner said, *"It should mean a strong and quick recovery. We are together. There will be no period of locating groups of Younglings from distant refuge points."*

She referred to the time after Hurricane Gigi when we distributed food from the humans to Brothers caring for Younglings. There were so few fish and crabs that many would have died without the help. I was as stressed as everyone. We were all in bad shape.

I said, *"I agree. There are few signs of distress among our Brothers. It is a good sign."*

Archimedes said, *"We need to consider how use of the shelter impacts us. I don't want the Nest dependent on humans."*

Archimedes was my mentor. His advice had guided me throughout my life. But with thoughts of terror when we dispersed to the deep reef edge to survive Hurricane Gigi, *this was better.*

Learner said, *"What is your concern? We only use the shelter in times of a great storm. The shelter doesn't change who we are."*

Archimedes said, *"At the last meeting, Brothers approached the Council asking to use the shelter for meetings and instruction of Younglings."*

Learner said, *"I can understand the request. The storm shelter could be useful."*

Archimedes said, *"The Council considered the request and approved limited use of the shelter as a trial. Then the Brothers realized the central location was not ideal, so they asked if smaller structures built along the reef slope to protect against predators."*

Runt's colors flashed through a ripping sequence of greens and yellows, indicating a mixture of humor and tension. *"I was at the meeting, and we were not sure how to respond. It was true. If small structures were placed on the slope, the Brothers would have protection from predators as they cared for eggs and Younglings. We thought it might strain our relationship with humans if we asked too much."*

I said, *"I think they would do it if they could, and would tell us if they could not."*

Archimedes said, *"I expect you are correct. But we need to be careful. Once the Brothers and Elders use human technology, it will be difficult to go back to not using it. Humans seem very dependent on their tools."*

I asked, *"Do you worry we will depend on humans too much? Or will we become dependent on technology, like humans?"*

"The two are connected," Archimedes answered. *"Technology comes from the humans."*

I could understand his concerns. Runt and I met with Mark and Jerry for a weekly lesson on human society. The topic of how technology influenced human culture was often our focus. Technology was a part of every part of human life.

I said, *"Humans would call these small shelters 'houses.' Mark says humans used to use natural caves on land for shelters, much like we use caverns in the reef."*

Runt said, *"I agree with you. We should be careful about adopting human technology without considering negative effects on the Nest."*

"Exactly," Archimedes said. *"If we use human shelters, the explorers will have no reason to look for new Nest sites. We would end up with too many Brothers on the reef and slow down the spread to new reefs."*

I asked, *"Did you explain your concerns?"*

"I did, but the Brothers were unconvinced and are continuing to ask that we approach the humans, asking for more shelters."

Runt said, *"The Council must ask for time. We need to consult with the humans."*

I said, *"Tell the Brothers that humans say too much metal on the reef can hurt the corals. Limit them to use of the existing shelter."*

"Is this true?" Archimedes asked.

I looked at Runt. His colors were dark, and his ridges pulsed. He knew I was pushing the limits of what Mark had shared with us.

"I will ask for more information at our next meeting, but, yes, Samantha and Mark have shared with us that metals react in salt water, and their use needs to be monitored."

Runt still looked uneasy, so I continued, *"Metal rusts when it is in salt water. That is why they have us look at red areas or where holes form."*

"Is rust dangerous? Are we damaging the corals?" Archimedes asked again.

"The humans have not said this, but their concern made me wonder. I will ask for more information. But for now, you can say we are concerned enough to want to limit the use of metal on the reef."

Runt said, *"Even if metal is not a danger, we need to be careful when we choose to use human technology. I value our ways of life. The more Charlie and I study how humans live, the more I am convinced that we must carefully choose what we adopt and leave behind."*

"*What are your thoughts on the use of shelters? Should we not use them?*" Archimedes asked.

I looked at the smooth, shiny walls again. The shelter was keeping us safe from the storm. Was that a bad thing? How did you decide what to adopt and what to walk away from?

I said, "*The humans brought the shelter because they value our presence on the reef and want us safe. We value our friendship and our communication with humans. That is why we have a strong presence on this reef. However, we must consider how many octopuses should remain in this Nest. The Brother's proposal to build more shelters would increase our numbers here.*"

Archimedes considered my message. "*We have more Brothers here than we ever had at one location. We should split the Nest before we overburden this reef.*"

Learner said, "*That will be hard. No one wants to leave this Nest. The interactions with humans make this Nest unique.*"

Archimedes said, "*Some Brothers can be persuaded, and we can limit the number of eggs we nurture. They will meet after this storm has passed. I ask that you both be present.*"

Chapter 29 ~Samantha ~What's Next?

Heron Island, Austraila

To my relief, the pregnancy test was negative. I was sure Peter was relieved, too. We weren't planning on kids soon. *Did I want kids at all?* I was very young during the great floods, and it wasn't fun and didn't leave me with positive feelings about childhood. We had been climate refugees living in shelters. Mom and Dad held things together. We had food and a place to sleep, but I had nightmares about the camp for a long time. And, I wasn't sure if the earth needed more people.

Peter knew how I felt. We discussed it before we got married. At the very least, we agreed to table the topic until we were out of college, with both of us working toward doctorates. He hoped I would change. But the thought of being pregnant here in Australia—away from home— frightened me.

I tried not to be too relieved about the negative test. Susan warned me that if I was in an early pregnancy, the test could give a false negative. She wanted me to wait a week and then repeat the test.

Dr. Snyder said no diving until the doctors knew why I passed out. He was right. People drowned if they passed out underwater. They wouldn't let me go out on reef walks away from shore. I was stuck with lab work while Peter took my place on the reef communication project.

They were sending me to Brisbane for diagnostic testing. Susan mentioned some terrifying possibilities, including brain clots. I told them it was most likely low blood sugar, but they wouldn't let it slide. I was sad and embarrassed. It felt like way too much was being made of me passing out.

"Samantha, are you busy?" Peter asked.

"No, just thinking about the research agenda. It's hard to have the team diving without me."

"You'll be back on the project soon. What direction do you want me to take for the vocabulary exchange?"

I said, "I've been following Blue's lead. He focuses on a fish, coral, or objects, and we exchange names for the dictionary. Like Charlie, he has an impressive memory and doesn't seem to forget a name once we've agreed on one."

Peter nodded and started to say something but paused.

"You have good instincts and a great team to work with. You'll be fine."

"That's not what I'm nervous about," he said.

"Then what?"

"Samantha, if you are pregnant, what do we do?"

"I don't think I'm pregnant. Let's not go there."

"What if you are?"

"I don't know. I'm hoping I'm not because I don't want to go through a pregnancy while I'm at a research station here in Australia. We haven't even decided if we're going to have kids."

"We might need to move our discussion of kids up. I know we weren't planning on it now or here, but people have kids in Australia. The medical system is world-class."

"Oh, come on! We're living on a field station. Both of our families are back in the States."

He looked so serious that he didn't look like Peter. He was one of those people who was always smiling, but there wasn't a hint of a smile right now.

"Okay, we don't have to talk about it right now. You're right. It's unlikely that you're pregnant. The implant is safe and effective, and I agree this isn't a great time or an optimal place. And I am worried about what caused you to black out. But part of me gets excited about the idea of a baby. So, if you are pregnant, we should talk about our life plans and maybe make some adjustments."

"I think it was low blood sugar. People are making way too much of this. I ran late in the lab and missed lunch before heading out on the dive."

"You're saying I can't trust you to eat if we don't eat together? That's bad."

"I won't make that mistake again. I'm paying for my carelessness. It stinks not being able to dive. Can we talk about something else?" I asked.

"Sure."

"My current work schedule includes two hours a day of reef time on the shallow flat, but for now, I'm not supposed to be in any water alone. Can you work your schedule to make room for a reef walk around low tide?"

"I'll talk to Even and Jim and see if they work the dive schedule to avoid low tide. It might take some doing, but they should be able to work with it."

I said, "We've been meeting with Blue at high tide for consistency. You should be able to go with me at low tide. It'll be like old times on Coastal Eleven."

"Yeah, they were good times. Weren't they?" he said.

"Yes," I said. "They were great times."

Chapter 30 ~Blue ~ Peter On The Team

Heron Reef, Australia

The humans came at the usual time. The shadow of their boat moved across the reef, and strong vibrations announced their entrance into the water. We watched as two humans moved through the blue water down to the patch of sand we used as a meeting space. One human unrolled the mat onto the sand. This mat was how the humans cast color sequences to communicate.

To my surprise, the human by the mat this morning differed from the one I was expecting. This human was larger, and the way it moved in the water was less fluid. There were other differences, too. I was sure this was not Samantha, the human I had become comfortable working with. I glanced at the second visitor, who remained apart to observe. That human had been here before. Only the one by the mat was new. The differences were difficult to see, and I could be wrong.

"This human is larger than Samantha. Do you think they sent an Elder?" I asked my mentor.

"Maybe. But this could also be a female," he replied.

I signaled agreement. Female octopuses were larger than males, and maybe humans had the same pattern.

I added, *"This one has a different shape, and the head projections are shorter. Maybe these are differences between male and female."*

He signaled agreement, saying, *"It is frustrating that we have so few words to work with. There are many questions to ask."*

"That is why we are here, and they are waiting. I should start."

Moving close to the sand patch and positioning myself for today's interaction, I pulled two pieces of rubble into places and sent a color sequence, *"Welcome, humans."*

The visitor exchanged vibrations with their companion and then responded.

"Welcome. Are you Blue?"

"Samantha called me Blue and explained about names. What should I call you?"

"Peter."

"Welcome, Peter."

We fell into our work. Peter would point to a fish or coral, and I would provide the color and movements we used to name the animal. It was the same way of exchanging information that Samantha used. We needed more than names for communication! I directed our attention to motions, and we added floating, jetting, swimming, and walking to our vocabulary.

Progress was good, but I wanted more information about humans and the differences *between* humans. Asking questions was so tricky. *How can I do this? How do I get him to give more information about humans?*

I held up my tentacle and showed the lack of suckers, hoping Peter knew that octopus males have one tentacle without suckers. I signaled, *"Male."*

Peter signaled that he understood. Then he tapped his head and signaled, "Human," then, "male."

"Peter male, Samantha female?" I asked.

"Yes," he responded.

"Octopus males are smaller than females," I said.

Peter said, "Human females are smaller."

"Is Samantha shape that of a female?" I asked.

"Yes," he replied.

"Will Samantha return?" I asked.

"Samantha can't dive now. She will come when she can."

A sad thought came to mind, and I asked, *"Is Samantha laying eggs?"* *Then I wondered, do humans lay eggs?*

"No eggs," Peter said, and I felt relieved.

I moved to the second visitor a short distance from where we worked and pointed.

"Human name?" I asked.

"Jim," Peter said.

I signaled acceptance and asked, *"What other words should we share today?"*

We worked together, adding many, many words to our shared vocabulary. I was glad my mentor was with me to practice what was shared. The head projections were called *hair.* According to Peter, most males had short hair, and many females had longer hair. We worked on numbers and distance. It was challenging, and I wasn't sure I understood everything Peter shared.

We watched the visitors rise through the water toward their boat and disappear.

I turned to my mentor. *"Humans name everything. They even gave me a name."*

"I see value in naming. It makes communication clearer," he said.

"Samantha named me 'Blue' because of our color. But we can't both be called blue. What name would you like?"

He was still considering a name for himself. It was a strange idea, but appealing. *How did humans find names?*

"I will think about it," he messaged.

Some Elders were better thinkers than me. I needed to ask for help.

Chapter 31 ~ Samantha ~Mainland

After my second negative pregnancy test, Dr. Snyder arranged a medical appointment for me in Brisbane. Until I was cleared for diving, I'd be stuck in the lab, so I was eager to get it over with. Peter came with me, which was good. I was terrible at navigating an unfamiliar city.

The five-hour train from Gladstone to Brisbane was uneventful but also tiring. When we arrived at the university lodging, all I wanted to do was freshen up and relax, but we were met by two zoology faculty members who asked us to meet them for afternoon tea.

Jeff and William were first-year research associates. They were young, funny, and friendly. Jeff had a beard and talked with a heavy Queenslander accent. William was from England and was dressed in well-pressed slacks and a business shirt. We sat together while we shared tea, and Jeff briefed us on the tangled web of trams, monorails, and moving sidewalks.

"You look confused," William said at one point.

Peter had been taking notes. He stopped writing and said, "I think I'm following your directions, but I'll tell you, your accent is a bit hard to follow."

William laughed, and I saw he had dimples. "That's why I'm here." Professor Baxter thought Jeff might need a translator.

We all had a good laugh.

When we headed out the next day, the streets were packed with people.

I hadn't had much experience in cities and being in crowds left me uneasy. I tried not to cling to Peter. For once, I was happy Dr. Snyder insisted Peter come with me on this trip.

The medical center looked like the ones back home, sterile with an intimidating atmosphere. I never liked doctors and would rather be just about anywhere else. Not for the first time, I wished I were home—back at Coastal Eleven. I missed seeing Charlie, Mom, and Jerry, and I hated how far away home was.

"Sam, what's wrong?" Peter asked, taking my hand.

"Being here in a doctor's office waiting. I don't like doctors."

He laughed. "How can you have a degree in science and be anti-doctor?"

"I spent a lot of time in the hospital with Dad at the end. You know, when he had dengue fever. I don't like to think about it."

"I hadn't thought about that. Sorry. I was just a kid, but your Dad was always nice to me around the lab. I forgot he died of Dengue."

"It's okay. Thanks for being here. We'll both feel better when we have some answers."

When the door opened, a petite red-haired young woman came in, smiled, and offered me her hand.

"Hi, Samantha, I'm Dr. Felice. How are you feeling?"

"I'm good. A bit nervous."

"Don't be. I've been reviewing your lab work and imaging, and I don't think you have any serious problems. Relax"

"That's great," I said, breathing a sigh of relief.

"We can rule out pregnancy, the lab test is negative, and there are no signs of cysts or an ectopic pregnancy."

Peter said, "That's a relief, but Samantha has never blacked out. Do you have any ideas?"

"Samantha, your blood sugar levels are alarmingly low. Your medical records show you've dropped almost five kilograms in less than a month. Are you trying to lose weight?"

"No, I don't even know how much I weigh. But I figured it had to do with blood sugar. I forgot to eat lunch that day."

"Yes, don't skip meals. You were in the low range for 'normal' weight when you left the States. Sometimes, people gain or lose weight when they travel. It can be because they don't do well with local foods, or because their normal routine is disturbed. You shouldn't lose any more weight, and you need to regain some of the weight you've lost."

"I thought it was just low blood sugar. I can be more careful about not missing meals and eating what's in front of me."

Peter asked, "So you think it's nothing more than not eating enough and missing meals?"

She nodded. "The test results point to minor malnutrition. Your blood glucose is low. You have mild anemia. I noticed you're also mildly dehydrated. I'm having our nutritionist plan a shopping list and a diet for you. Do you eat cheese or drink milk?" she asked.

"Sure, when I can get them," I said.

"I want you to eat cheese, eggs, fish, or one of the protein products every day and to follow the portion size suggested by our nutritionist. I'll include a list of recommended multivitamin supplements."

"That's it?" I asked.

"That's it. At least for now."

Peter said, "Thank you. We're relieved the problem isn't serious."

"Well, let's not ignore the issue. Eating disorders can be serious. I'm sending a scale back to Heron for you. I want you to step on the scale every day."

"Why?"

"The scale will send your weight to our database. That way, I can monitor changes in weight without you making the trip to Brisbane."

"Can I go back to diving?" I asked.

"Hold off another week. I want you to eat well for a week, and we'll run another blood test. You can visit the clinic in Gladstone to give a blood sample. The data will go straight to your records. As soon as you're no longer anemic and dehydrated and your weight is stable, I'll clear you for diving."

I nodded. "I can do that."

Dr. Felice stood, shook our hands, and said, "It was a pleasure to meet you both."

I turned to Peter and said, "Let's get some lunch."

"Sounds great. Sally suggested a place at South End she thinks we'll like," he said.

It was a great place, across from an artificial lagoon bordering the Brisbane River. The white sand beach and crystal-blue water made it look like an authentic tropical lagoon. The restaurant was very nice. I had spanakopita, a delicious Greek dish with spinach and feta cheese. Peter had a local favorite: meat pie.

Having an artificial lagoon right next to a natural river might seem strange. But the river had large bull sharks. No swimming in the river. The lagoon was a good idea and was quite beautiful.

Chapter 32 ~ Samantha Lagoon

Six of us gathered tanks, regulators, fins, and masks in a flurry of activity. Peter, Joe, and I would be on the dive team heading out to meet the octopus colony, and the boat would be full. The other three divers would enter with us and then work a transect line sampling coral, looking for genetic markers to identify bioengineered corals. We would meet back at the boat.

I had a gorgeous day for my first dive in over two weeks: a cloudless blue sky and water like glass. I felt better than I had for some time. It wasn't only the weather that put a bounce in my step. The clinic's diet had helped. My appetite at mealtimes had improved, and I didn't feel like I needed a nap anymore. My energy levels had definitely improved.

The clinic scale showed my weight inching upward, which might have been unnerving, but it wasn't. Mom had constantly fussed at me, saying I was too skinny and I needed to eat. I guessed she was right.

Dr. Snyder waved me over from outside the equipment room.

"You're looking good. Excited to be back on the dive team?" he asked.

"More than you can imagine."

"Peter tells me you're ready to try the avatar again."

I nodded. "I've been reviewing Charlie's recommendations and I want to try some ideas . I think the forced break in fieldwork was good for my creativity."

"Good. Hopefully, Blue won't head for the hills again."

"Charlie had a good suggestion. Ease into it by showing an image with a word on the display mat. If Blue responds well, we'll present a static image of the avatar with the word avatar. The idea is to let him see that an image of a fish isn't the fish, and an image of an octopus isn't an octopus."

Dr. Snyder said, "It's great you could consult Charlie. You make a good team."

"I know; we've been friends for almost eight years. It feels like forever."

"Eight years is a long time. I thought the Caribbean octopus had a lifespan of three years."

"Charlie's part of a population we call the Nest, and we think they are a new species, or on their way to becoming a new species. It looks like the bioengineered corals and expanded reef system fueled rapid evolution. We've tried to ask about lifespan, but they seem not to know. Charlie was a Youngling when we met—about a year old. He's considered an Elder now. To my knowledge, only Charlie's mentor, Archimedes, was older. I don't like to think about losing him."

Dr. Snyder nodded. "Hopefully, it won't be for a long time. I see your team is ready to haul equipment to the boat. I won't keep you."

"Thanks for stopping by. I'll let you know how it goes."

The team was leaving the equipment room when I joined them. Jim was pulling a canvas cart loaded with fins, weights, masks, snorkels, and wet suits. Peter pushed a steel cart with a built-in rack securely holding six scuba tanks. I fell in next to him and helped pull the cart.

We were heading to a shallow reef on the north end of the lagoon. It was a popular snorkeling site with abundant sea life in shallow water. We needed the tanks to stay by the mat on the sea floor to process information during the exchange.

The use of artificial intelligence made our work possible. But we still needed to respond and direct the flow of information. We needed stay for an extended time on the sea floor. So we used tanks and dealt with carting all the gear to the boat.

When I first met Charlie, I didn't know how to use scuba. Charlie was less than a year old, and we met on the reef flat in extremely shallow water. He approached me after watching me work with corals. He was incredibly patient and didn't give up.

Our work here was different. We humans approached the population of octopuses trying to open communication. We didn't assume they would work with us on our terms. Scuba made it possible to work at a depth they found comfortable.

The time spent with Dad walking the reef flat were cherished childhood memories. I still loved walking in the shallows and watching life move around me. Snorkeling brought me face to face with the amazing reef creatures and filled me with joy. But learning to scuba dive truly opened the world to me. Being able to hover motionless and be part of the underwater world made it possible to focus on details and the subtle nuances of behavior. I didn't think I really appreciated how complicated and beautiful the reef ecosystem was until I learned to dive. I'd missed diving these last two weeks and couldn't express how excited I was to be heading to the doc with the team.

"Do you have everything?" Peter asked.

"I do. Let's go."

I stepped beside Peter, who was pulling the wagon behind us, and we headed down the pathway to the dock, avoiding muttonbird nest holes as we walked. I still couldn't get used to birds digging holes for their Nests.

We left the shade of trees and stepped onto white sand, with the harbor's glassy blue water stretching before us. Fifteen minutes later, we were on the water speeding toward the lagoon. By seven fifteen, we tied the boat to a mooring buoy, donned our gear, and slipped off the back of the boat. Peter and I drifted down to a patch of coral surrounded by sand. Blue and two other octopuses waited for us.

Peter unrolled the mat and attached my tablet. It came to life, and he initiated a greeting color sequence. "Hello, friends."

A rainbow of colors passed over Blue's head and tentacles, and a clear voice sounded into my earpiece, *"Greetings, Samantha and Peter."*

I looked at Peter. He had a regulator in his mouth and goggles over his eyes, but I could still sense his smile. His eyes were bright and happy. When I couldn't dive, he assumed the responsibility of maintaining progress. He had more than delivered. Now, it was my turn.

I took the position in front of the mat. I typed in a command onto the control tablet. A detailed vibrant image of staghorn coral appeared on the display mat. I typed the next command onto the tablet, and a sequence of colors moved like a banner beneath the image. Charlie had suggested I return to working on building vocabulary, and that was what we'd been doing for almost a month. During that time, we'd used the display mat strictly to deliver color sequence when pointing to fish or other organisms on the reef.

Today, we would try to get the octopuses to recognize images displayed on the mat—a step I should have taken before introducing an avatar and scaring Blue away.

I worked my tablet, and a lifelike image of staghorn coral appeared on the mat. Below the image, I sent the sequence we had agreed upon for the coral.

Blue remained uncharacteristically still. One of his companions exchanged a color sequence and movement of tentacles, and in my earpiece, I listened to the computer voice intoned, *"What?"*

I repeated my color sequence and pointed to the mat, which still had an image of staghorn coral, and then pointed to a piece of staghorn coral on a reef outcrop. I repeated the color sequence and waited.

Blue pointed to the image, then to the piece of coral. The color sequence flashed across his tentacles, and the voice in my ear intoned *"staghorn coral."*

Yes! Blue had accepted the image and made the connection to the name.

He and Gray pulsed and moved their tentacles, an action that I took as excitement.

Peter gave me a thumbs-up.

I cleared the display and initiated an image of a parrot fish.

Blue responded with the same sequence, *"parrot fish."* As he did so, in my earpiece, the beautiful words, *"Parrotfish,"* came through.

I held my breath and adjusted the tablet. The image of the avatar was displayed on the mat. Below the avatar, I sent the sequence for "Samantha two."

Would he understand?

Chapter 33 ~ Blue ~ We Try Again

The water was calm as the boat approached our meeting site. My mentor, Gray, was with me, and we watched the divers enter with a splash, slide down to the edge of the reef, and set their tools onto the sand.

It was Peter and Samantha by the mat. We moved into position. This time, Gray stayed by my side. When the mat came on, it seemed to have a piece of staghorn coral in it. Then, the color sequence for staghorn coral moved across the bottom of the mat.

I didn't know what to make of this. How did they have staghorn coral in the mat?

I messaged, *"What?"*

Samantha pointed to a piece of staghorn coral near the mat.

"What is the human doing?" Gray asked.

"I think they are working on vocabulary a new way," I responded.

"Staghorn," I messaged to Samantha, pointing first to the coral and then to the mat.

The staghorn in the mat disappeared, replaced by a parrot fish.

The fish wasn't swimming, but there was motion. The fins moved gently, the way they do when a fish is hovering in place.

"Do they have a captive parrotfish?" I signaled to Gray.

"I don't think it's a real fish," Gray said. He moved to the mat and touched it with his tentacle. *"I think the mat makes the fish just like it*

142

makes the colors."

We watched a sequence of colors flash across the mat below the fish. It was the same sequence we used to name *parrot fish*. Then, the fish seemed to swim across the mat, disappearing as it reached the edge of the mat.

"*Why would they show us this?*" I asked Gray.

The fish had reappeared in the center of the mat and almost seemed to be watching us.

I stroked the mat too. The fish looked real, but when I touched the mat, it was flat like the sand. *The fish wasn't really there.*

"*How can I see but not feel the fish?*" I messaged to Gray.

"*I don't know,*" Gray messaged, but it seemed they wanted to work on language.

How could a fish in the mat help with communication? But if Samantha and Peter were trying to communicate, I would try. "*Parrot Fish,*" I signaled, repeating the color sequence Samantha used.

The mat darkened, and then another creature appeared: a small but tasty crab. Like the parrot fish, the crab stayed in one place, but when I looked closely, I could see parts of the creature's mouth and antennae in motion.

I signaled, "*Coral clinging crab.*" It was the name Samantha used for this type of crab.

I couldn't help myself. I touched the place on the mat with the crab. It was not there.

"Yes," Samantha signaled and repeated, "Coral Clinging Crab."

She continued showing creatures on the mat. I continued providing names. Gray and I watched as corals, sponges, sea cucumbers, and a large variety of fish with names briefly appeared and disappeared.

Then she stopped and moved a short distance away from the mat. She was near Peter, and I felt vibrations and watched them communicate.

When Samantha returned to the mat, she gave a new color sequence.

"Pictures," and showed all the creatures we had just named. When the last creature was gone from the mat, she showed the sequence again. "Pictures."

The word was new: *Pictures.*

How could all these creatures be called pictures?

I felt excitement move through me, and my ridges pulsed.

"Any creature in the mat is a picture!" I messaged. *"When the mat shows a creature, it is like us using colors to mean the creature! "*

"Maybe," Gray messaged. *"Let's see what the humans do next."*

I thought I understood, but not fully. *Why use a picture instead of colors and movement?*

I messaged, *"Yes. Pictures."*

Then, the captive octopus appeared on the mat, and under it, the message, "Picture."

My ridges pulsed, and I saw that both Gray and I were dark and still. When the captive octopus moved, signaling a greeting, I wanted to flee. But I didn't. Gray was signaling to me, *"Communication."*

So I waited.

The captive octopus disappeared, and the message "Picture" appeared on the mat.

I remembered my terror at the "captive" octopus and could feel the colors of shame on my head and tentacles.

It wasn't a "captive." It was a *picture* of an octopus, and Samantha wanted to use the picture to communicate. I thought I knew how she would use it. The idea was exciting, and I felt my ridges ease and my colors lighten. A glance at Gray told me that he, too, was excited.

"Picture?" I messaged.

"Picture," Samantha answered.

Then, the picture moved its tentacles and signaled, *"Hello, we greet you, friends."*

Chapter 34 ~Samantha~We've Got This~

Peter and I sat on the bow of the boat. With the other divers in the back, it felt like we were truly alone. It was a bit bumpy and windy on the deck with my back against the wall, but at that time, it felt like the world was perfect. The salty smell of the ocean filled me with a sense of home. Peters's arm, strong and reassuring, rested against my shoulder. I wanted the trip to the reef slope to last forever.

"A penny for your thoughts?" Peter said.

"Just feeling how wonderful it is to be here with you, on the water. This is a beautiful day, and life feels perfect. I'm also relieved."

Peter shifted and pulled me closer. "About the avatar?"

I felt the warmth of his knees next to mine. It was surprisingly intimate.

"The avatar and other things."

"The pregnancy test?" he asked.

I nodded.

He said, "We should talk about the test results. We haven't discussed starting a family since before we decided to get married."

"I had mixed feelings about having kids then, and I still don't know if I want kids," I said.

"Sam, I'm glad you're not facing a pregnancy here. We are far from home and don't have a support network. But I won't lie. One day, I would like us to start a family."

"Peter, my father worked as a researcher for NOAA, and his work changed the world. That's the life I want, and I'm afraid I can't have that and raise children."

"Your father had kids."

"Yes, but mom didn't pursue a career. NOAA hired her to do technical work because they stationed her with Dad. It was convenient. Her work was necessary. It still is, but it's a job, not a career. I've thought long and hard about this; I want a research career."

I looked at Peter and asked. "Are you volunteering to downsize your career like my mom did so we can raise kids?"

He didn't answer for a long time. "Until last week, I would have said no. But, when I thought you might be pregnant, I was excited. It surprised me how excited the idea made me. So yes, I can adjust my career and make it work."

"That is good to know," I said, losing some of the tightness in my chest. "We will revisit the topic, but for now, I'm not ready. I don't know when I will be."

Peter looked hurt, and I struggled to find words to soothe without agreeing.

"Okay, we don't have to have a date on a calendar, but it's a topic I want us to come back to. And I'd like us to think about our plans for after Australia, and consider when having a child might fit into our plans."

"I've been thinking about what comes next," I said

"And?"

"I need to formalize a doctorate topic. All my coursework is just about done; it's time to formalize a dissertation topic."

"Charlie?" He asked.

"Well, the Nest will include Charlie. I want to do a behavioral and cultural study. Maybe have it jointly supervised by Zoology and Anthropology."

"I think that's a great idea. You could map it out while we are here and send proposals to the faculty. You'll likely have a supervisor lined up before we leave."

"I'm going to need to improve my skills with the avatar," I said.

"You're going to use the avatar to expand interactions with Brother and Elders, aren't you?"

"I am."

"You should write and send it to Dr. Kelly; he'll likely find financial support from NOAA for your study. You'll need to work with the anthropology department to make sure you're on solid ground, but it's a great proposal."

"The Elders have been pressing you for lessons on human society and governance. It puts me in an excellent position to ask them to share details of their social structure. I think I can publish a few articles while I work toward the dissertation."

"I can see us taking over the little cottage. You'll likely need to be at Coastal Eleven for extended periods."

I nodded. "I'm hoping this isn't just me being homesick and wanting an excuse to be at Coastal Eleven."

"Does it matter? Part of your motivation can be a desire to spend time at home. Remember, it isn't just your home. It's the home of the next, the most exciting scientific discovery in recent history. It's a suitable dissertation topic, and you are well qualified and situated to complete the research successfully."

I could feel the engines slow and looked up to see we were approaching land. I snuggled in next to Peter, enjoying the comforting security of his arm over my shoulder. The boat slowed and guided into the harbor. Peter and I stood up to help with lines to secure the boat at the dock.

The sky was a vivid blue with no trace of clouds. The sun warmed my arms, and I felt alive and well. I felt better than I had in a long time. The world felt right, like everything was going to be okay. *Had I been depressed? Did the thought of being pregnant scare me that much?*

We hadn't talked about what would come after I completed my doctorate. I want to talk to Mom about it. Mom and Dad had children years before Dad worked for NOAA. He had his doctorate and was a professor before the floods. Mom had a bachelor's degree in Earth Environmental science. She had kids and didn't continue her education. Peter's view of compromising on "our" career path and having kids is what Mom did. She supported Dad, raised a family, and still works in science. It wasn't a bad compromise, but it isn't what I want.

We can think about a family after we both have finished our doctorates.

Chapter 35 ~ Blue ~ Conversation

Heron Reef, Australia

Gray's theory felt right. Humans had an image of an octopus and were trying to communicate using the image. We were eager for the humans to come so we could test the theory. The idea of any creature communicating was strange, but humans were from another world.

Gray was beside me and messaged, *"I want you to engage the image as if it were an octopus from another reef."*

"Why me and not you?"

"I want to observe."

"I understand, but I might ask for help."

"What kind of help could I give?"

"Help me know what to say."

"Try to think of the image as a Brother from far away. Ask questions you would ask of a traveler from far away."

"Should I ask about where they are from and what the conditions are like?"

"Yes, that would be a good start. It would be good to know why humans are here."

That helped me relax about the meeting. It was good that my mentor was with me.

A shadow moved across the sand. On the surface, a boat approached the reef wall and stopped. Three creatures entered the water and moved down to the sands. The one we called Samantha unrolled the mat, and an image of an octopus appeared before us.

It felt strange, but I did as Gray asked. *"I greet you, traveler,"* I messaged.

A sequence of colors moved across the head and tentacles, and the image deftly moved the tentacles in response. "We greet you and thank you for accepting this image so we might communicate."

"It is a wonder to be able to message to others. To beings that are not like us," I messaged.

"It is for us, too. We have exchanged information with octopuses like you at our home, but it is still new. Every contact is exciting and important."

I considered the image before me. It seemed so lifelike that it was easy to forget I was dealing with a construct—something humans made to communicate with us.

"Why now? Humans have never approached us before."

"Until we met our octopus neighbors, we did not know there was life to message and talk with us in the ocean."

"That is fair. We didn't know humans communicated, but I am not surprised. I've watched humans on the reef. They work together, so they must communicate."

"Human communication is very different. So different we have to use complicated technology to talk to octopuses."

"Like the octopus image?" I asked.

"Yes."

I decided not to think about the technology and just talk to these humans. *"Humans are land dwellers. Do you have Nests like ours but on land?"*

"Yes, our Nests are on land. We raise our young and work together to secure food and protect each other."

Accepting that these creatures, who were so different from us, and also like us, was difficult.

"You were prepared to meet us? You came looking for us?" I asked.

"Yes, Our Nest is far from here. Humans travel far. One from our Nest was on your reef and observed you. She felt you were intelligent and could communicate. We came to see."

"Not all octopuses message," I said. *"We have others who are like us but silent."*

"Not all octopuses at our home reef message," the image communicated.

"Do all humans communicate with each other?"

It took a while before the image responded. "Yes, all humans communicate. There are many languages, and sometimes, we can't communicate with each other."

"When we have visitors from far away, messaging is difficult."

I looked at the humans next to the display mat and reminded myself that these were the creatures I was talking with—not the image in front of me. The thought made my ridges pulse with excitement.

"Yes, your messaging differs from the octopuses we know at home. That's why we had to share words and learn your messaging."

The image on the mat was still giving me time to consider.

"Why do humans come underwater? Even before you came, humans have been regularly on the reef."

"Humans know the land and ocean seem separate, but they are not. Humans have always been curious about ocean life, but now we know that the ocean's and land's health are linked."

"I don't understand your words."

"Our shared vocabulary is still limited, and I'm not sure we have enough words to explain. But I will try. Do you know white coral?"

"We have seen white coral. Sometimes, if many corals are white, the fish leave.

"Back home, we work with our octopus friends. We treat white coral to help it heal. The octopuses find white coral; humans have medicine to treat coral."

"We rarely have any white coral. When it comes, it goes away quickly."

"We know, but we worry that the white coral will someday be a problem here too."

"And, what is this medicine you use?"

"Special food that helps coral recover."

"It is good to know humans can help if our reef needs help," I said. "But for now, I am excited to meet with creatures so different who wish to share information."

Chapter 36 ~Samantha~ Reflections

They said that all work and no play made a person dull. But nope. I've always been better when I was working—happier and surer of myself. Peter told me I needed to get better at leisure activities and learn to have more fun. But what could be more fun than being on the reef? And if I was on the reef walking, snorkeling, or diving, I was making observations and trying to piece together what I'm seeing. *Is this reef healthy or stressed? Is this a coral that I've seen before? Are there octopuses I can talk with?*

Yeah, the last one came up a lot.

Dad was a biologist, and I grew up living on a research station off the coast of Georgia. The island had been part of the mainland before the great floods, before the bioengineered corals spread through Florida and Georgia. Our island had white sand beaches, a reef flat, and a lagoon. When I turned ten, Dad started taking me on his daily reef walks. Just thinking about those walks made me happy.

Dad died when I was twelve, and I felt like my life ended. I've spent almost half my life without him. But when I was on a reef, it felt like he was with me. *I wonder how he would feel to know I'm on the Great Barrier Reef, talking with intelligent octopuses.*

He'd be pleased that his bioengineered coral project worked even better than his team had hoped and that reefs had spread north and into deep waters. And, as they had hoped, the reefs were sucking carbon dioxide from the atmosphere.

My family lost our home to the rising waters of the Atlantic. Dad's work gave humanity the promise of a more secure world. I didn't think Peter would consider having kids if we still had constant storms and floods. I still had nightmares of our life in the climate refugee camp. *Is that why I'm so nervous about having kids?*

"What are you thinking about? You look a million miles away," Peter said, bringing me out of my reverie.

"Bioengineered corals and carbon sequestering," I said.

Peter laughed but didn't look happy.

"What? We're knee-deep in a coral lagoon. Why shouldn't I be thinking about corals?"

"Well, I'm thinking about being knee-deep in a coral lagoon on this magnificent island with my beautiful wife." He moved over, took my hand, and squeezed it.

I could feel myself blushing and returned the squeeze. "I was also marveling at how much Dad's work has changed the world and how successful the bioengineered corals have been. We wouldn't be discussing having kids if the waters were still rising. So, I guess I was thinking about us and the possibility of having kids."

Now his smile was back. "I like that better."

I pointed to the massive reef flat before us. "I want to experience as much of this reef as possible while we're here. Heron Island is so far away that we might never see it again once we leave."

Peter said, "It looks a lot like Coastal Eleven. I have to keep reminding myself we aren't back in Georgia."

"It took me a while to notice the differences." Pointing to the red organ pipe coral, I said, "We don't have this in the Atlantic. For every species of coral back home, there are at least ten we don't have."

"Yeah, it's funny that the reefs still seem so much the same. I don't see the diversity because I don't know enough to recognize all the species."

"The differences are subtle, but once you learn to recognize corals, you see that the reefs here in the Indo-West Pacific are amazingly diverse. For example, back home, there are only two species of Acropora, with over 300 species in the Pacific."

"Sam, whenever I talk about reefs with you, I get overwhelmed. It feels like my head will explode."

"Oh, come on, I'm not that bad." *Well, maybe I am. When will I learn to keep my inner nerd in check?*

"Why are there so many more species here?"

"The Indo-West Pacific reefs are much older. Biologists favor an evolutionary theory with corals evolving in the Indo-West Pacific and migrating outward from an epicenter. Not all species made it to the Caribbean."

"Wait, were the oceans connected?"

"They were until two or three million years ago, when plate movements formed the isthmus of Panama, separating the Caribbean Sea from the Pacific Ocean. Since the separation of the oceans, the diversity of corals in the Caribbean Sea has been decreasing."

"Do you think the new bioengineered corals will increase diversity in the Caribbean?"

"Part of me wants to say I don't think so. We only have twenty-three species of bioengineered corals. That isn't enough to make a difference. But, over evolutionary time, two or three million years? Who knows? Particularly if we keep adding new species. We might have started a new evolutionary center."

"When will you talk to Dr. Stevenson about your doctorate proposal?" Peter asked.

"I have a call scheduled for five this afternoon. That will be eight am in New Savannah."

"Does he know you're proposing a study that crosses zoology and anthropology?"

"He does. I emailed him a synopsis, and he thinks it's a worthwhile proposal. He wanted an online Zoom meeting to discuss a timeline and potential faculty supervisors."

"Wow, you didn't waste any time."

"I'd like to have an approved proposal and supervisor in place as soon as possible. I've been drifting too long."

Peter pulled me in for a kiss, then glanced at his watch. "It sounds very cool to me." He reached for my hand and squeezed it.

I wondered if he realized I had sidestepped the topic of kids again. We would have to talk about it sooner or later, and I needed a better handle on what I wanted.

Chapter 37 ~ Samantha ~Trouble

Heron Island, Australia

I used a flashlight and worked my way through the Pisonia thicket at a snail's pace. During my first week on Heron, I tripped in a muttonbird hole, landed on my bum, and had to go into a meeting covered in mud. I was more cautious now. It wasn't night, but the sun was low enough that it was hard to see the burrow holes.

My mood was not the best. I'd spent an hour trying to connect with Dr. Kelly. We had an appointment to discuss my dissertation proposal, and the internet connection wasn't working. I tried to shake it off. Peter was cooking dinner, and Sally and Jim were joining us. They didn't need me to be a killjoy.

"It smells amazing in here. You're making curry?" I asked.

"Yes. Jim caught some small wire-mouthed groupers. They're too small for baked fillets, so I figured a nice fish and vegetable curry would be nice."

"Yum. What can I do to help?"

"Check the rice and set up dishes of cucumbers and yogurt?"

"I'm on it," I said and checked the pot. The rice was on simmer. I tasted it and added a pinch of salt. "Have you been in touch with the lab today? I tried reaching Dr. Kelly but couldn't get through."

"We haven't talked since last week, and now that you mention it, I haven't seen the normal weekly report. It usually comes in on Wednesday. Did you call on the satellite phone?"

I nodded. "When I couldn't get through with the teleconference software, I tried the satellite phone. It rings, but no one picks up. I couldn't leave a message. It doesn't have a voice mailbox. "

"That is odd. Try sending him an email. Let him know there might be a problem with the satellite phones."

"I did that yesterday. He hasn't gotten back to me."

Peter moved the cast iron pan from the stove and tasted the curry. He looked up and said, "That's not like him. Let's reach out to Alana. Maybe she knows what's up."

"I'll do that. Alana and I text all the time. She's keen on keeping up with our progress. But now that you mention it, I haven't heard from her for a few days."

"Hi, guys," Jim called as he marched in carrying a bottle of wine.

Sally followed him, brandishing a plate of cut vegetables, cheese, and crackers. "Wow, it smells amazing in here," Sally said.

"It's all Peter tonight. He's a better cook than me," I said.

"Jim's contribution of grouper inspired me," Peter said.

"Yeah, only Peter could figure out something to do with fish that small," Jim said.

"Hey, have you been using the internet or satellite phones?" I asked. "I think we might be having a connectivity issue."

"Funny, I was going to ask you the same thing," Jim said. "Emails to the University of Queensland are going through fine, but a few emails bounced when I sent them to Berkeley in California. Weird."

Sally said, "I talked with my brother in England this morning."

Peter said, "Connectivity seems to be hit or miss. Sam, try again in the morning."

I nodded, feeling uneasy. *Was I being a worrywart?*

Jim said, "Interesting. We seem to connect to England, but not to the

United States."

"Did you use one of the resort landlines to call England?" Peter asked.

"Yes."

Peter nodded to Sally. "The landline is old school—it's a radio signal sent to a tower in Gladstone, then fed into the phone system infrastructure."

"Maybe." Jim said, "But it's also the nature of geosynchronous satellites. Maybe the satellite was in the right place to connect to England, but not the United States."

I sat down on a stool, feeling a little shaky. It could be a coincidence that Jim couldn't get through to colleagues in Berkeley, but it felt like a big coincidence. Right now, home, Mom, Jerry, and Charlie felt very far away. It took every bit of restraint not to leave, get the satellite phone, and try calling Mom. Without thinking, I stood up.

Peter must have read my mind. "Sam, you can't call now. You'll scare your Mom. It's two am at Coastal Eleven."

I sat down again. "Okay, let's open that bottle of wine."

Sally must have thought that was a good idea. She pulled the bottle opener and served us wine. I was not a big fan of wine, but I'd make an exception tonight.

Chapter 38 ~ Charlie ~ Disappearance

Coastal Eleven, Georgia Barrier Reef

As we moved close to the reef wall, a school of fish scattered. But we were not here to hunt. We moved through an aperture and passed through the winding pathway of coral and rock into a chamber. The light was dim, but soon, my eyes adjusted. Archimedes, my mentor, and Menech, the Senior Elder, were waiting for us. Archimedes approached us and signaled for us to wait. Soon, the remaining Elder Council members joined us in the chamber.

Menech addressed us first, *"The humans missed meeting with you?"*

I signaled agreement. *"But what is more concerning is that humans are no longer visiting the reef flat. They seem to have disappeared."*

Menech asked, *"Are there no times when humans are absent? Have we been keeping track of human movements on the reef?"*

Archimedes said, *"Human visitors are frequent and many. This absence is unusual."*

I watched the exchange between Menech and Archimedes. The light sequences were complex and difficult to follow in the cavern's darkness, but I sensed that Menech was not convinced the Nest needed to take action.

Archimedes addressed us, *"Is there an action you would have us take?"*

"Yes, we should take shelter. The only times humans leave the island is

when a great storm approaches," Runt said.

I could see my tentacles darken, and Archimedes noticed. *"Charlie, I see you disagree with Runt. Share what you think."*

"Jerry and Mark would have warned us before leaving for a storm, so I don't think a storm is approaching."

Menech said, *"Do you say we should not take shelter?"*

I said, *"We should move Younglings to the storm shelter, but not a full evacuation."*

Menech asked, "If it is not a storm, why might humans leave the island?"

Archimedes said, *"Charlie and Runt shared from their lessons that humans face dangers from other humans and have complicated governance systems."*

"Do you think there might be disagreement with the human Elders on working with us?" I asked.

"It could be that," Archimedes said. But his colors were dark, and his ridges pulsed. It looked like he was holding something back.

I asked, *"You think it is something else? What do you suspect?"*

"Charlie, you have shared that human disagreements often involve violence. You told us about 'countries' and 'wars.' I do not understand human culture, but what you shared was alarming. What if a conflict between human countries is at fault? Could war be why they are no longer on the reef?"

Could this be? My heart was heavy with worry.

Chapter 39 ~ Samantha ~ Is anyone there?

Heron Island, Australia

After two hours on the phone, Dr. Snyder had some answers, but not many. What was certain was that no one in Australia had been in contact with anyone in the eastern United States in the last forty-eight hours, and communication with the rest of the world seemed unaffected.

The University of Queensland sent Professor Baker from their Department of Political Science/Public Relations to Heron Island to help us understand the current situation. I almost laughed. Peter was in the same academic program. But I couldn't laugh. It was far too serious.

Dr. Baker arrived in the late afternoon and asked us to wait until morning to meet. I was unimpressed, but Peter said it was what he would have done.

"Why?" I asked.

"He's been traveling all day, and he's been out of touch. Things happen fast in politics, and I'm sure he'll spend most of the night tracking information so he can share the current state of affairs with us in the morning."

I didn't get any sleep, and I doubted that Peter did. When Dr. Baker arrived for our eight am meeting, the entire research staff was in the conference room waiting. The room went silent as he walked in and moved to the front of the table.

He was a small man, middle-aged, and the only one in the room wearing a tie. At least he wasn't wearing a jacket. If he was intimidated by the intensity of our crowd, he didn't show it.

"I'm going to share what we know with you. Please understand we are still trying to piece together information and facts. There are theories about what has happened, but I'll hold off on those and share what we know."

We held our questions, waiting for him to continue.

He turned the display on, and a map of the United States came into view. The map showed that New York, Washington D.C, Virginia, and states south of Virginia to Florida were darkened.

"Communication to the Southeast Coast of the United States is down. The affected areas lack electrical power. Phone and internet communication have been disrupted. The government sent people from Nashville to travel east into the affected regions. They reported chaotic conditions and a complete lack of electrical power."

Peter asked, "Was it an EMP attack?"

"We have to be careful about using the term 'attack.' And we have to be careful about calling it an "EMP." It appears that devices were detonated that were *similar* to EMPs. Call them EMP 2.0, and yes, they caused the damage."

I said, "How in the world could it be anything other than an *attack?*"

"Well, in 1989, a solar flare caused an EMP that knocked out power in Quebec, Canada and caused power issues in the United States. But in this case, the prevailing theory is that this was a deliberate act using very sophisticated devices that caused electromagnetic pulses, and disabled computer chips."

"Why the East Coast?" Jim asked.

"Peter, we need to go home," I said. "How quickly can we arrange transportation?"

Dr. Snyder looked pained. "Samantha, right now, your folks would want you to stay here, safe."

Peter said, "Sir, I agree with Sam. We should try to get home. We can't just hide out here."

After an uncomfortable silence, Dr. Baker spoke up, "The question is academic. The entire world is in a state of high alert. The United States has temporarily grounded air traffic. At the moment, trains are holding in the terminals as well."

"Why?" I asked.

Baker rubbed his neck and consulted his tablet. When he looked up again, he addressed the room, but it felt like he was looking straight at Peter and me.

"Keep in mind the event happened only five days ago, and American policy is changing rapidly. The American government declared a state of emergency with martial law on the day the power grid collapsed. That included an international travel ban. Two days ago, they began letting foreigners return home *if they could find transportation*. While they haven't said international vessels can't dock, no countries are sending their ships into what could soon be a war zone."

Peter reached over, took my hand, and gave it a gentle, reassuring squeeze. It helped some as I tried to hold back tears that were about to break free. When I looked at him, he was as rattled as I was. This wasn't something we had ever considered possible. We worried about the rising sea level, storms, poachers, and idiots who damaged our reefs. We were worried about the octopuses and how our species would work together in the future. Attacks on America? War? It wasn't in our vocabulary. *Where did this come from?*

"Why would anyone do this? And why the East Coast?" Dr. Snyder asked.

"That's the question," Baker said. "We have strategy and political experts in Sydney, London, and Maryland who are floating a wide range of ideas. Everything from foreign interests trying to cripple the military to an act of insurgency from within disaffected citizens."

We let that sink in for a minute. Around the table, I saw expressions of horror and disbelief. Peter and I were the only Americans in the room, but Australia had strong ties to our country, and our fates were very connected.

"The New York City lost power at ten forty-five am on September Twenty-ninth. It appears a powerful ground-level EMP device detonated in Grand Central Station. Shortly after that event, a cascade of solar power station failures occurred, spreading through the New York boroughs. Four hours later, the power in Washington D.C. went down."

"They must have used the train system to deliver the devices," Peter said.

Baker nodded. "It seems obvious now, and people agonize over the lack of action. But, no one had ever employed a ground-level EMP device with the range of this device. This really is brand-new technology. They think the device launched at the train stations when the carrier pulled into each station to exchange passengers and cargo. What also hurt us was that each detonation cut the location from communication with the rest of the world. It was days before the pattern of train delivery became obvious. By that time, power was down all along the southeast coast."

Dr. Snyder said, "A ground-level EMP would only affect equipment in a small area. How could the whole East Coast be dark?"

"The experts tracked the time solar stations shut down, and it follows wind patterns from the time of release. One theory is that we are seeing nanobot technology of sophisticated miniature EMP devices. One theory is that the initial detonation launched a small rocket carrying a payload of nanobot EMP transmitters-small and light enough to be carried in the wind. Evidently, some of them are still airborne and still transmitting." Baker stopped talking.

I had so many questions that I didn't know where to start.

Yes, I did. "You said the international community isn't allowing ships to travel to the United States. Why are they cutting off the unaffected areas like the West Coast?" I asked.

"Good question. And I'll tell you, Americans are not happy about what they feel is a lack of support. However, the Australian commission officials worry that another attack would disable any ships in port. An EMP disables the computer chips that deliver energy from the storage batteries. And, if the local solar array is disabled, Americans won't be able to supply charged batteries for a return trip."

Baker added, "EMPs destroy computer chips, so virtually all the computer systems and any electronics that use computer chips are gone. The current theory is that Washington, DC and New York were the primary targets, and the other cities were the targets of opportunity."

I stopped following the discussion. Peter was the policy and political person in the family, not me. Family. All I could think about was my family in Georgia—Mom, Jerry, Mark. All I could think about was: were they okay? How were they coping? And that I needed to get home.

Chapter 40 ~Charlie ~ Searching

Coastal Eleven, Georgia Barrier Island

I curled a tentacle around the base of a sea fan and tried to adjust my gaze away from the blinding sunlight. We were in the shallows, where small fish darted between rocks and corals, moving so quickly that their colors blurred. The water was shallow and warm, uncomfortable for us, but humans often walked here from the beach. So we came here to search for signs of humans.

This reef flat wasn't unknown to me. When I was very young and sent to explore, I met Samantha not far from here. Many Younglings were sent exploring, searching for sites to claim for a new Nest. This process eased crowding and spread our Nest to new reefs. I was proud to be given the responsibility of exploring.

I remembered the excitement I felt, entering the lagoon for the first time and discovering it was rich in food and that the reef crest was shallow enough that sharks and other large prey animals wouldn't be able to enter the lagoon. The Elders quickly agreed to move to the new site. It was here, during those explorations that I met Samantha. I was very young, and as I watched her work with coral polyps, I thought she was trying to use them to communicate. I became so excited that I approached her and tried to exchange messages with her.

I was wrong. Humans did not communicate by sign language using coral rubble. But it was a momentous meeting and the beginning of the partnership between humans and the Nest. It took many tides, patience, and the miracle of human computers, but we developed the means for humans and Brothers to talk and work together. The reef was better today because we worked together.

So, where have they gone?

Once again, the Elders had sent me here, not to look for a new Nest, but to look for humans. The mystery was maddening. There had been many tides and light and dark periods since Mark and Jerry visited the meeting site. Samantha was far away in another country—Australia. If she were here at Coastal Eleven, I would feel confident she would reach us. *Will Mark and Jerry find us?*

Maybe, but I didn't have the same confidence.

The signal device seemed to be working. When we pushed the signal button, the light changed from red to green, but no one came. Archimedes reasoned that maybe the boat was broken, and humans could not travel to our deep-water meeting site. He sent Runt and me to the shallow site, remembering that we still had a signal device in the shallows, although we had not used it since Samantha and Peter began using scuba at the reef slope site.

We found the signal device easily, but pressing the button did not give a red or green light. I pushed the button anyway, even doubting it would send a message. Maybe the device was too old. We moved through the shallows, hoping to find Jerry or Mark or evidence that humans were still on the island. This was where humans were likely to enter the reef from the island. If they did, we would see them.

I lingered at the site today, thinking of when Samantha and Jerry walked out and searched for us to warn of a great storm. They came after other humans had evacuated the island, even though staying put them at risk.

Because they were brave and warned the Nest, we took shelter, and no lives were lost. Had the humans evacuated again? Or was Archimedes right, and they could not reach the deep-water site?

For now, we looked for humans, not just Mark and Jerry. Many humans knew of us and would recognize our actions as attempts to communicate, even if they couldn't understand us. Samantha said the octopuses of the Nest were famous now.

I hoped we would find them soon. It had now been longer than I could remember without human contact. The situation was uncomfortable.

Chapter 41~ Samantha~ Who Did It?

Heron Island, Australia

Twenty-four hours later, we were back in the conference room, and Baxter was updating us. None of us had slept, and tempers were barely in check.

"The good news is that there have been no additional acts of aggression," Baxter said.

"Does that make sense? Who would do something like this and then just stop?" I asked.

"I say it is good news because it is looking less like an act of war and more like an act of terrorism," Baxter said.

Peter asked, "Is anyone claiming credit?"

Dr. Baker said, "No credible group is claiming credit."

Peter said, "If it was an EMP, that means the trains are down, correct?"

"Well, trains that were in the affected area were left disabled. Because there might be some nanobots still in the atmosphere, it's risky to send more trains in. That situation will resolve itself over time, but even if they were able to send trains in, all the solar stations were destroyed. The people in charge do not want to risk more damage, so right now, travel between cities is by foot, horse, and non-electric bicycle."

"Jesus," Peter said. "They think there might be additional attacks."

Baker said, "They don't know but don't want to risk additional equipment. It will be difficult to replace or repair what they've already lost. But, the nature of the attack was such that the experts are ruling out calling it an act of war."

"Why?" Dr. Snyder asked.

"Countries wouldn't be able to effectively send an invasion force. Their equipment would shut down when they entered."

Peter said, "I'm not convinced it couldn't be an act of war. They could be taking the long view. They could be planning an invasion in the next few months when the nanobots are all grounded."

Baker said, "Well, the pundits don't rule it out, but they say it's unlikely. They would have an insanely hard time supplying power to troops."

"Can we communicate with Cuba?" I asked.

There was silence while everyone looked at me. *Okay, my mind takes strange leaps.*

Dr. Baker opened a computer and checked something. "The northern tip of Cuba was hit, but not all the country. The experts think the EMP launch in Orlando was close enough for some nanobots to end up there. The northern tip is only about 160 km from Florida."

Peter moved closer and put his arm around me. I don't know why I thought of Cuba, other than once again, I was in a foreign country with no way home and only Peter for support. That wasn't fair or true. These people were not our enemies, and we were not keeping us from going home. They just weren't able to help us get home yet.

"Do you have friends or family in Cuba?" Dr. Baker asked.

"Colleagues," Peter said.

"I'm sure they are fine."

"How are the West Coast and central states reacting?" Peter asked.

"They are scrambling to harden as many of their systems as possible against attack—no one thinks this is over. In addition, they are sending food and supplies and technicians to rebuild systems."

"Using horse-drawn carriages?" Peter asked.

Baker nodded. "Using what they have," he said.

I was beginning to grasp the full seriousness of the situation. Without trains, sending food into the affected area would be difficult. People could starve, particularly in towns with large populations. Suddenly, I felt comforted by the knowledge that Mom and Jerry were on Coastal Eleven.

They could set up a distillation station and purify water, even without solar power. Mom and Mark were scientists. They could figure it out. They might get sick of eating fish, but they wouldn't starve. People in the heart of Atlanta wouldn't be as fortunate. Peter would be frantic about his folks. They didn't even have a garden.

"Any idea when we can expect communication to be restored?" I asked.

"The supply carriages carry satellite phones to deliver to local government seats. All the existing satellite phones will have been destroyed, but new ones won't be affected."

The table went quiet. We were all lost in thought, trying to process Baker's information. It felt surreal.

Dr. Snyder said, "I know it's hard, but there isn't anything we can do from here. It doesn't help if we sit around stewing about what's happening. So, in the meantime, I'm suggesting we continue our work. Our work was important yesterday, and it will be important tomorrow. Do you have any questions?"

The table was silent as everyone considered Dr. Snyder's words. Then Jim from our dive team spoke up. "Dr. Snyder, I'd like to ask for some personal leave. The ferry to Gladstone is tomorrow morning. I want to check in with my family in Brisbane."

Dr. Snyder took a while before answering. "How long of a leave do you want?"

"I'm not sure. Long enough for the tensions to ease. If Australia is attacked, I don't want to be caught away from my family with no means to reach them."

I looked around the room, wondering how many others would ask for leave.

Then Dr. Baker spoke up. "I understand your concerns. What I can tell you is that the government is working to ensure the protection of transportation systems. It's unlikely the same kind of attack would be successful."

I looked at Jim. He didn't seem convinced. *How do you protect against an EMP?*

What I knew for myself was that we couldn't go home right now. So, for us, Dr. Snyder was correct. Our work was important, and we needed to return to the reef and continue working on building a relationship with Blue and the local Nest.

Chapter 42~ Arrival

Coastal Eleven, Georgia Barrier Island

Jerry bounded up the stairs and pushed into the kitchen, where Amanda and Mark sat with coffee. The sun's light masked the lack of electricity, and Jerry glanced at the camp stove Mark had stationed on the counter.

"Mom, there's a boat offshore. It looks like it's heading to the harbor."

Mark spoke first. "What kind of boat?"

"A sailboat, a big one with two sails."

They had been without communication from the mainland for over a week since the power went out.

"Well, it's about time someone came to check on us," Amanda said.

"I'm nervous that it's a sailboat," Mark said. "It means the power outage wasn't just local."

"That's what I figured," Jerry said.

"Well, at least we're about to get some news. Come on, let's say hello," Amanda said, gulping the last of her coffee.

Mark stood and shook his head. "Stay here. Jerry and I will see who it is."

"What? Why can't I come?"

"We don't know who they are. I don't expect trouble, but our house is fairly well hidden. I hope it is someone we know, but I'd rather you stay here until we see that they are people we know. Or that they at least seem friendly."

"That's ridiculous. What do you think they are after? Our buried treasure?"

"He's right, Mom. We don't have any news from the mainland. We don't know how they are handling a power outage. I've been a little glad we are about here alone."

"Amanda, they could be looking for food and shelter. If they are folks we know, that's fine. Until we know more, I'd like to be cautious," Mark said. "Whoever used an EMP did it to create civil disruption, chaos. People on that boat might not care that the house is ours or that we need our food to survive. It won't hurt to be cautious until we see who it is."

"I think you're being alarmist," Amanda said. "If they seek safe shelter and food, we won't send them away. And I don't know about you, but I want some news! I want to know what the hell is happening. Let's compromise. I'll come with you, but stay out of sight. If we know them, I'll join you."

Mark stayed quiet for almost a minute before giving in. "Okay, but stay out of sight."

Jerry said, "We have flare guns. Should I take one with me?"

Amanda said, "Stop it. No one is coming here to rob or murder us."

Mark shrugged. "Let's go meet our visitors."

They headed down the stairs to the walkway over to the harbor. Jerry detoured to the tool hut and stashed a flair gun. He avoided making eye contact with his mom.

They watched the ship tack back and forth toward the harbor. It didn't look like the captain experienced sail power, and it took them a long time for the ship to work its way into the harbor. Then, a familiar figure stepped off the deck and tied the line to the post.

Amanda pushed past Mark and rushed forward to hug the visitor.

"Steve, you have no idea how good it is to see you!"

Jerry was right behind his Mom. "Dr. Kelly, what's happened? What's going on?"

Before he could say anything, two more people—a woman and a teenager—emerged from the boat cabin.

Amanda met her on the deck and hugged her. "Sue, it's so good to see you. Is this your son?"

"Yes, this is John."

Dr. Steve Kelly said, "We should sit down and talk. I'm sure you have questions. I don't have all the answers, but I'll share what I know."

"Where did you get this boat?" Mark asked.

"Let's go up to the habitat," Amanda said, "I'll put some tea on."

Thirty minutes later, the six sat at the kitchen table, sipping tea.

"Sorry, we don't have any milk," Amanda said.

"This is wonderful, just as it is. What are you using for fuel in the camping stove?" Sue asked.

"Wood," Mark said. "This is a high-efficiency camp stove. We had a store of hickory wood to use, but I've gathered local wood and set it to dry. This stove will burn just about anything."

"Okay, everyone is comfortable. Steve, bring us up to date. Steve, we are guessing this was an EMP attack. What can you tell us?" Mark asked.

Amanda said, "Was this an attack? Are we at war?"

Steve said, "At first, that's what everyone thought. But then, no one followed up with an invasion, and no country claimed credit. It's still possible, but for now, the government is treating the event as a terrorist attack."

"Who would do that?" Amanda asked.

"Good question. It seems we've been on a vacation from terrorist attacks and fear of world wars. Everyone's been so focused on navigating climate upheaval that folks seemed unwilling to waste energy on fighting each other," Steve said.

"How much damage?" Jerry asked.

Whoever did this used the railroad system to deliver devices to cities on the East Coast of the United States. Everything from New York down to Florida, including Washington D.C. So, things are a wild mess."

"Atlanta and New Savannah?" Jerry asked.

"Yes," Steve said.

"How bad is it in Savannah?"

"Bad enough that I'm hoping you won't mind if Sue and John stay here for a while. Without power and transportation, food shortages are already starting to be a problem, and it could get bad enough for violence to break out. I figured you would be safe. I brought additional supplies."

Sue said, "You didn't say you were leaving. You can't do that!"

Steve reached over and took Sue in his arms. Then he turned to Mark.

"When I saw my neighbors stockpiling food and weapons, I decided it was time to get my family to safety. I can't stay with you just yet."

Amanda put her cup down and said, "Steve, I'm uneasy about not having any way to get to the mainland. Yes, we can fish and won't starve, but I'm not sure we can sustain life long-term here. I'd feel a lot better if you and the boat stayed."

"I agree you need transport. I'm hopeful it won't be long before our boat's motor is replaced and Captain John will be able to provide transport. If that doesn't happen, I'll have him bring this boat back. "

"Why can't you stay?" Mark asked.

"I didn't wait to bring Sue and John out here. Family comes first. But I'm also part of the emergency response team. It's my job to keep things from getting bad in New Savannah. We all have friends in the community that we want to survive."

"No," Sue said.

"No? What do you mean, No?"

"I mean, we aren't staying here without you. If you go back, John and I are coming with you. We leave the supplies here, but we go back."

"Sue, let's take a walk and talk about it."

Chapter 43 ~Blue ~Understandings

Heron Reef, Australia

By the time our humans returned to the reef, sunlight made the sea fans and corals pop with color. Darkness, and the predators of the dark were gone for now. The bright light eased my tension. We, too, were predators, and the instinct to hunt was strong. Gray and I had already eaten, so I let the crabs move undisturbed across the rock rubble and sand.

Soon humans arrived, spreading their mat onto the sand. As Gray predicted, the false octopus once again appeared on the mat. Now that I had expected the image and knew that humans had constructed it, I could easily see the differences between the image and the fish swimming in the water before us.

I messaged Gray, *"I am embarrassed that I thought this image was alive."*

"The humans are clever. When the image moved, it seemed to be alive. I was fooled as well."

We watched the two humans. The larger male moved to the side and worked with a device that extended far above the sand, pointing it at the mat.

Samantha, the female human, did something to the device, and the image of the octopus moved. Now that I knew she controlled the image, it was apparent that Samantha's actions connected to the movement. What amazed me was Samantha used her control to make the false octopus *message* in a way we could understand. The image used our language.

Gray and all the Elders were stunned. The exchange of motions and colors left no doubt they wished to know more about the humans use of our language, and they wanted me to seek answers. I wished I was not their point of contact. There were braver, smarter Brothers for this important work. But my chance encounter with Samantha left me in this uncomfortable position. The Elders counted on me. I had to control my fear.

Samantha worked her device, and the false octopus messaged, "May we ask questions about your community?"

I looked to Gray, who acknowledged with a motion that he did not know the term.

"What is 'community'?" I asked.

"A group of individuals who live together and share work and food. Usually, they share protecting each other, hunting, and raising young," the false octopus answered. "We see that you are with other octopuses. You appear to live in what we call a community."

"I think you can call our group a community. While we hunt alone, we all make sure young octopuses have enough food. We like to be alone at times, but we come together often."

"Humans and octopuses are different in many ways. Still, it is amazing how much we have in common. Humans also live in communities, share work and raise young together. We are rarely alone," the image said.

I reminded myself it was the female communicating, not the false octopus. The scene in front of me left me pulsing in excitement. These humans lacked tentacles and the ability to change colors for communication. How wonderful it was that they could make the false octopus deliver their messages.

The false octopus moved its tentacles and flashed a color sequence. It said, "Does your community have a leader or group of leaders who decide for the group?"

"We do. We have a group of five octopuses who are older and known for leadership. We call these our Elders."

Samantha seemed excited at the message. I watched as she and the other human exchanged vibrations. He, too, seemed excited. She considered this, and I watched as the image conveyed the message.

"You have much in common with our octopus friends back home. They call their community a Nest. I think it is because they first came together to raise their young. They also call their leaders Elders."

I thought about it and agreed, *"Nest is a good name for a group of octopuses sharing work and living together."*

Gray moved forward, showing he wished to participate in the communication directly. I moved aside for him.

Gray messaged, *"We are interested in knowing what you know of other octopuses who communicate. Many octopuses do not make messages. Is the community you know far from here? You traveled here, could they?"*

It was a good question, and I was glad Gray thought to ask it.

Once again, the humans exchanged vibrations. What an exciting way to communicate!

"It is too far for members of the Georgia Nest to travel here. But you might still be able to share information with them."

Gray messaged, *"More information."*

The fake octopus moved slowly as if considering what to say. I watched Samantha start working on the tablet, stop, and then start again. Each time she stopped, its image went still.

"I am controlling this avatar to communicate with you. We might be able to have our friends in the Nest, back in Georgia, control this avatar. I am uncertain if it is possible. We can try."

We looked at the fake octopus, what she called the *avatar*. I returned to the center position as Gray moved to give me space. *Could we learn to do that? It didn't seem possible.*

"*Is that the fake octopus's named? Avatar?*" I asked.

"No, avatar is a name for any image generated to communicate. This one has a name. We call it S.A.M."

"*Is that because you are named Samantha?*"

"Yes, the image is named for me since I was the first to use an avatar to communicate."

While I watched, Samantha had the avatar move a tentacle, then seemed to move across the mat. The effect was very real.

"*I think S.A.M. is a good name for this avatar. What do you call human communities? Are they also called Nests?*" I asked.

"Sometimes we talk about them as our Nest when communicating with our octopus friends. But when talking to humans, we call them towns or cities. Like octopuses, our communities need a place for shelter. Octopuses often use large caverns in rock formations and sometimes enlarge them. Humans build shelters from materials on the land."

"*Is this island a town or a city with shelters? How many humans live on the island?*"

"The island is like a town, and humans have built shelters. However, this town is also different. The shelters stay on the island, but humans only stay there for a short time, during a series of tide and sun cycles. Sometimes, only a few. Then they return to towns where they live, and other humans come."

"*Will you and the other human with you stay long?*" I asked.

"We will be here many cycles. Although we do not know how many. When we leave, other humans will communicate with you."

"*That is good. We have much to learn from you.*"

"And we have much to learn from you. Blue, we need to leave soon.

Humans can only remain underwater for a short time. We would like to meet again. When would be a good time for a meeting?"

"This time of sun cycle is good for us. Can we meet again after two cycles?"

"We call a sun and moon cycle, together, a 'day.' We will meet here again after two days have passed. At the same time of the sun cycle, which we call 'mid-morning.'"

"Agreed," I said.

As we watched, the image of S.A.M. disappeared, and Samantha rolled the mat up. Then, the two humans swam up to the boat and disappeared from the water.

Chapter 44~ Guests

Coastal Eleven, Georgia Barrier Island

Steve opened the gray case and unpacked a miniature solar array, setting it on the deck outside the kitchen. Amanda wondered how much power something so small could produce. When Steve folded the four panels down from a central battery, the unit was a square, less than a meter on each side. The design was elegant. The central battery served as a robust base holding four solar "wings" horizontal, a meter from the deck.

He pressed a switch, and a digital display showed 0.5 kWh.

"It'll produce more when the sun is higher. Obviously, you're not going to have electricity for the house, but it will keep your electronic devices charged."

The small device was a cube with four solar panels on hinges. Steve pulled the panels to a horizontal position. He pressed a switch and a digital display showed 0.5 kWh.

"Steve, we don't have any working electronic devices."

He reached into the case on pull a rugged satellite phone and connected it to a charging port.

Mark, Amanda, and Jerry stared at the phone and solar array, saying nothing.

Amanda said, "I guess we can call people outside the affected area?

Is it safe to use?"

Steve looked puzzled. "What are worried about?"

"I don't really understand EMP science. Will having it out in the open like this put it at risk?"

"We'll talk about the EMP blast and protecting the phone and power station in a bit. Let me answer your other question first."

He handed her a small notebook and said, "When I deliver a phone, I bring a directory on numbers for phones that have already been delivered, and another list of phone that are scheduled for delivery."

He opened to a page with a bookmark. "I figured you would want this one in Georgia State University. I know you have friends there. You won't be able to call anyone directly, you'll reach people who can tell you about conditions at that location. Hopefully, they can relay messages as well. This should help keep people connected until we have our normal systems running again."

Amanda picked the phone up with a tenderness that was almost a caress. "Steve, is life ever going to be normal again?"

"Amanda, what is normal?"

"Well, like it was before the EMP."

"It's a fair question. I don't know. Life changes. We aren't the same as we were before the great floods. We reached a new equilibrium, a new normal. It wasn't at all the same as before the floods, but different doesn't always mean bad. I mourn the people we all lost in the floods. I miss some of the things we took for granted, but our way of life isn't worse, just different."

Amanda nodded. "I see what you're saying, I don't miss constant advertising driving me to buy stuff I didn't need or want."

"Exactly."

"Some changes will make it easier for us to survive this attack. Cities are more food resilient today because population density is lower. Even in our cities, people have gardens and grow food."

"I don't know. Samantha and Peter didn't have a garden in Atlanta. I worry about Peters' family. They grew some herbs and a few tomatoes, but I wouldn't say they were food resilient."

Steve paused for a minute before continuing. "I'm not saying food is abundant. But, there haven't been riots. Most families had a small garden, and some even had chickens. People were terrified, but after a few days, tensions eased and people have been surprisingly good about sharing."

Amanda nodded. "Good to know, but I don't think we can count on the goodwill lasting long term. If they're primarily living on neighborhood gardens, they are on semi-starvation rations."

"It helps that almost every day another neighborhood has its power restored. The EMP blast only destroyed computer controller chips, so 99 percent of the array technology, including the actual solar panels, are fine. Companies in Canada and California are producing and shipping them out rapid fire. It takes time because the trains still aren't running in the affected areas. But people see recovery, and they can hold out."

The conversation slowed as everyone drank tea and processed the reality of the situation.

Mark asked, "How is distribution being handled? How do you get chips and phones in from Canada?"

"My contacts at the University of Quebec arranged the original bicycle convoy to bring phones with charged batteries. That was the start. Now, we have routs that include restored power. They are using electric vans for longer distance. I don't know all the logistics."

Amanda said, "Do they know who did it? What would stop them from doing it again?

Steve said, "Good question. Again, the officials are leaning toward the theory this was terrorists or hackers. As they repair solar panel controllers, they are installing Faraday cages. They had to use Faraday cages anyway because there were still nanobot EMP transmitters in the air. They seem to be grounded now."

Jerry asked, "What are they doing to find the terrorists?"

"I don't know the specifics of what the FBI and CIA are doing, but the United Nations issued a resolution of commendation to any nation involved with the action or helping any individuals involved in the attack."

"Did that do anything?"

"Well, international aid has been flooding into the United States. As of now, no one has claimed responsibility. If they planned on reaping prestige or gaining allies, it isn't happening."

Amanda put her coffee down. "I'm telling you, after all that humanity has been through, the flooding, loss of life, and uncertainty that we wouldn't go extinct, it's unbelievable that any group of people could do this. What the hell were they trying to do? What did they want?"

"Well, the United States has never had a shortage of enemies. At first, speculation was that the action came from a terrorist organization. But with no one credible claiming credit, it might be pranksters."

"They would go to jail for life," Amanda said.

Mark drew a breath in. "Maybe, but maybe not. They could land a rather cushy job."

"Come on, that's insane," Amanda said.

"No, Mark is right. We have a history of rewarding some ingenious and crazy pranks by giving people high-level jobs rather than jail time. At one point, I think the statistics were that one in four hackers ended up on a federal payroll."

"Do we have a death toll for this prank?" Amanda asked.

For a minute, the room was silent.

Steve said, "No, we don't, and it won't be a small number."

Amanda said, "I'm familiar with the history of hacking computer systems. But this is different. Computer hacking didn't kill people."

Steve said, "I don't know. The history of cyber attacks is filled with multinational hacks that affected millions if not billions of people. And, the experts think these assholes might not have expected all the devices would be deployed. They expected the train to be stopped.

"Why wasn't it?" Amanda asked.

"The first EMP went off in New York, leaving the city dark. No one connected the damage to the train route. With all the panic and confusion, they didn't connect the damage to a train route until long after the final EMP device was delivered and detonated."

"Jesus," Jerry said.

Mark said, "I'm guessing a bunch of security folks are looking for new jobs."

Steve said, "Yes, current thought is that the people who did this didn't expect to cause this much damage and are trying to disappear without claiming credit. The FBI, Homeland Security, and the CIA are all focused on cracking the case."

"I hope they are also working to prevent future attacks. Wouldn't want to recover just to have it happen again," Mark said.

"I hear you. Officials are working to harden communication equipment and power production stations against future EMP attacks."

Sue opened the door from the kitchen. "We have tea and campfire biscuits. Come join us."

Steve placed a Faraday cage over the power generator and phone and followed Amanda and Mark inside. The table had a plate piled high with biscuits and a pot of strawberry jam. He nodded appreciatively.

"I'm impressed with your camping skills. You seem to get on without electricity."

Amanda said, "We miss it, but we're getting by. Jerry rigged a campfire oven and bakes biscuits and flatbread. We don't have butter or anything that needs refrigeration, but we had a supply of jams on hand, and we've been using them sparingly. They have a high enough level of sugar that the osmotic levels prevent bacterial growth."

Sue looked perplexed. "I think I know what you mean."

Jerry said, "Yeah, this family speaks in science. It can get old. Anyway, the levels of sugar are so high, that bacteria cells would shrivel up and die. It's safe to eat."

Sue said, "Steve, how long will you stay on the island?"

"Just a few days. I want to go out on the reef with Mark and Jerry. But I'm working on the relief effort, and I'm needed."

"Steve, I'd feel much better if you stayed. When you leave, we have no way off the island," Mark said.

"It shouldn't be too much longer. Captain John has been working on rebuilding the electric motor. It should be operational soon. Now that you have a working cell phone, just call for pickup."

"You're sure the phone will work and won't shut down again?" Amanda asked.

Steve pointed to the gray bag. "Keep the phone in the Faraday cage with the power generator or in this bag. Both will protect it. I don't think there are any nanobot generators still in the air, but let's be safe."

"Can we call Samantha?"

"We can try. But let's wait until it's daytime in Queensland. I think it's three am right now."

Chapter 45 ~ Samantha~Long Distance

Heron Island, Australia

The shrill sound of the satellite phone filled the room where I had been napping, a concession to multiple sleepless nights. At first, the sound was so unexpected I didn't realize someone was calling. Then, I almost tripped over a chair, scrambling to get the chest of drawers open and find the phone. All while trying not to be too excited. It had been a long time since the phone rang with an incoming call.

I felt goosebumps on my arms, even though I knew it was almost certainly a call from Brisbane or from people on the West Coast of the United States. I was desperate for news about Coastal Eleven, New Savannah, and Atlanta. Peter reached people he knew in California, but the news Peter had scraped together was fragmented and disheartening. People in California knew almost as little as we did.

"Hello," I said into the phone.

"Samantha, thank God. I'm using a new type of satellite phone, and I wasn't sure if I'd be able to reach you in Australia."

His voice was, as always, strong, calm, and reassuring. The world could be ending, and Dr. Kelly wouldn't have a hair out of place. That wasn't a helpful thought. It was an EMP attack. The world might be ending.

"Dr. Kelly, Is Mom okay? What's happening at Coastal Eleven?"

I took a breath, waiting, reminding myself that a delay was normal for the overseas satellite call.

"They're fine. I'm calling from Coastal Eleven now. I'll put Amanda on in a few minutes. She's kind of emotional right now."

I could imagine Mom breaking down. She cried at the strangest times.

"Tell Mom I love her."

"I have you on speaker," he said

"I love you too, sweetie," Mom said.

I swallowed hard, then said, "Dr. Kelly, what's going on? We hear there was an EMP attack.? Do you have any information for us?"

"You might have access to more news than we do. With no internet or television, we aren't getting news. My colleagues in Canada say the blasts were along the eastern coast," Dr. Kelly said.

I said, "That's what we heard. We also heard they used nanobot technology with micro transmitters that stayed airborne and continued transmitting. "

There was silence on the line.

"Are you still there?" I asked.

"Yes, and I was right. You might have as much or more information as me," he said.

"How did you get to Coastal Eleven?" I asked. "I mean, the boats run on electric motors."

He said, "I took a university sailboat. It's a longer sail than I've ever done, but the boat handled the crossing fine. I came with supplies, and I'm also leaving Sue and John here. With the chaos in New Savannah, I've asked Amanda if they could be guests."

"You're not staying?" I asked.

"No, I have work to do. Mostly distributing satellite phones and power stations like the one I brought here."

My mind was trying to process new information, but I was feeling better talking with Dr. Kelly. Hearing Mom was okay took a huge weight off me.

I asked, "How did you get a working satellite phone?"

There was silence on the line, and I wondered if the connection had been lost.

Mom said, "Sam, are you and Peter okay? I've been so worried."

"We are fine, just worried about everyone back home."

Then Dr. Kelly's voice started again. "Samantha, it's a long, complicated story that can wait. The short version is about finding a working landline and contacting colleagues in Toronto. They shipped a case of them to Nashville. Then a bicycle riding club arranged a network of riders to make the 800 kilometer journey."

I said, "That's amazing. It's difficult for me to imagine anyone riding a bike that far." I could hear a gasp from Mom, and for a second, Jerry's voice came through. Then Dr. Kelly continued.

He said, "In normal times, it wouldn't have been that hard of a task. But with the chaos and violence breaking out, it was quite risky. Yes, the riders were impressive young men. The first riders brought twenty [five phones with extra charged batteries."

I had a million questions about how he arranged this, but they would wait for another day.

Mom said, "Samantha, I can't tell what it means to hear your voice. I miss you so much, but I'm glad you are where you are and that you're safe."

"Mom, Peter, and I are fine, but I wish we were home. It's killing me to know what everyone is going through with us so far away."

Dr. Kelly said, "Samantha, Amanda is right. Things might get ugly for a while in the cities. We are fighting food shortages. There are parts of the cities that are powder kegs. We have less to worry about knowing you are safe."

"Dr. Kelly, I'm trying to wrap my brain around what you're saying, and I know that Peter and the rest of the researchers here will have questions and want to talk to you as well. Can I go get the others?"

"Sam, that's a good idea. Why don't we take a break and talk again in an hour? That way, you can get Peter and others from your team. It would be good to share information. As I said, people in Australia are likely to have insights that I don't, and I can fill you in on conditions in ground zero."

"Okay," I said, and listened as he ended the phone call. The silence was suffocating.

"Sam, I'm sure you and Peter are agonizing over what's going on here. We are going to be alright. And call me Steve. Everyone else does."

"Okay, Steve. We will wait for your call."

Chapter 46 ~ Charlie~ Contact~

I was right. Three humans were in the shallows. I moved onto the sand patch and flashed colors to announce my presence.

"Hello."

Their feet were in the water, and everything above the water was distorted. These might be the humans I knew. I was not sure. I waited, but there was no response to my message. I sent a new message, *"We were worried for you."*

The humans were aware of me. They pointed at me, and I felt the familiar vibrations they used to communicate with each other. It was frustrating that I could not understand what they said.

I tried again. This time, I used a formal message and placed pieces of coral on the sand, asking, *"What is wrong?"*

Now, one placed a tablet on the sand and positioned rock fragments to form an *X* over the tablet screen. Was he telling me the tablet was broken? *Then, why does he not use another tablet? Humans have many tablets. If this is Mark and Jerry, who is the third human?*

They were male and knew I'm trying to communicate, so that might be them. My ridges pulsed, and my colors flashed. I worked to calm myself, wishing they were in the water instead of standing. I couldn't see them well enough to know who they were.

As if he knew my thoughts, the human bent and lay flat in the water. He had a mask on, looking directly at me. It *was* Jerry, and I reached with a tentacle and stroked his arm. Contact was made, although we still were not communicating.

He arranged pieces of rubble on the sand, and with excitement, I realized this arrangement was one I had used with Samantha long ago before we had an operational translator.

He was asking me to be patient. At least, I thought that was what he was asking.

I wish I knew more about humans! Why isn't Jerry using a tablet or mat?
***

Jerry stood after arranging the coral pieces.

"What did you say to Charlie?" Steve asked.

"I used a pattern of rubble pieces from Samantha's journal. Charlie used it with Samantha when they were working on the translation dictionary. It's incomplete since I can't send color sequences. But I'm hoping Charlie recognizes it. It was part of a message asking for patience, the message says, 'We are working on it.'"

"That was smart," Mark said. "You studied her journal last night?"

"I couldn't sleep and remembered her old journals were still on our bookshelf."

"Jerry, are you saying Samantha wrote down the color sequences she used?" Steve asked.

Jerry said, "Yeah, she was thorough with keeping her journal, even as a fourteen-year-old."

Steve added, "Her dad trained her, and he was the most meticulous journalist I knew."

Mark asked, "Steve, can the computer team program this cell phone?"

Steve said, "No, right now, the only phones with the program not fried by the EMP blasts are in Australia with Samantha and Peter."

"Are we working on getting a local phone with the program?" Mark asked.

"The Georgia Tech folks want to help but are occupied fixing their own problems. Without electricity, they can't do much, and all their backup programs are inaccessible. In short, until the campus has electricity and operational computers, we can't access the programs."

"When we can talk to the Nest, how do we describe or explain this?" Jerry asked.

"I don't know," Steve said.

Chapter 47 ~Samantha ~ Conference

Heron Island, Australia

Dr. Kelly gave me an hour to gather those who were interested in an update from Georgia. That was everyone—even folks not on the research team. I didn't know some of them, but I thought they were tourists staying at the resort on the other end of the island. Anyway, the conference room was so packed we had to ask people not on the team to stand against the wall and let our team sit at the conference table.

"Peter, why are so many Australians here? Is it just morbid curiosity?"

"That's part of it, but the attack scared everyone. It happened in America. It could happen here."

Dr. Baxter added, "There are reasons for the interest. The United States owns most of the communication satellites we use here in Australia, and we depend on America for defense resources. Australians might not express why America is important to them, but they know it is."

We sat in silence, waiting for Dr. Kelly's call. When the phone rang, Peter stood and pressed the button, engaging the system.

"Hi, Steve, you have many people excited about this call."

"Great to hear your voice, Peter. Want to fill me in on who's here for the phone call?"

"We have quite a crew here. First, we have the research team and station staff. There's a resort on the island. So, we have some of the staff and visitors from the resort who want to listen in. I hope you don't mind. Sam brought up some of what you told her, but everyone here has been crazy for lack of news."

Steve said, "I'll do what I can to fill gaps, but understand that I have a fragmented knowledge of the situation. We're still without dependable electricity, and we don't get news. I'll answer questions that I can."

Baker opened the questions, "Can you bring us up to date? For example, tell us how civil order is being maintained?"

"The National Guard has been working with local police to enforce a curfew and rules about travel. At first, it was to prevent looting. Now, they also help out with mundane things like bringing supplies in for community gardens and distributing staples like rice. Most people are grateful the government is trying to keep them safe."

Peter asked, "Steve, who do they think did the attack?"

Baker was listening, taking notes. I wondered if the call was being recorded. The room was so quiet I had to look to see if people were still there. They were hanging on every word in silence.

Steve said, "There are many theories, and not much information is being released. The officials are saying they don't want to jeopardize an ongoing investigation. I think the answer is that when they catch them, we'll know."

Baker said, "Samantha shared with us about the bicycle couriers bringing satellite phones and computer chips into the southern coastal states. How fast is power being restored?"

"I don't have the big picture, but here in Georgia, our solar stations are dispersed and relatively small. Each station supports roughly five neighborhoods spanning a ten-to-fifteen kilometer range. Every week, at least one station goes on line. I suspect the holdup is transporting the technicians capable of replacing controller chips into the panels. And of course, Georgia would be in competition for people and materials with the rest of the affected regions."

Baker asked, "What are they doing to protect against additional attacks?"

"Great question. I'm not sure I'm the person to ask. I'm sure they are putting safeguards against this particular threat, maybe hardened computer chips. But, that won't mean we are protected against the next time someone decides to throw a monkey in the works. So, I don't know."

We had to think about this for a while.

I said, "I know you're planning to leave Coastal Eleven in a few days. How long will you be gone?"

"I need two weeks. I'm part of a team delivering satellite phones to re-establish connections between isolated populations. I had coverage for now, but people are counting on me."

Peter said, "You brought your family out to Coastal Eleven. Is that because you're worried about outbreaks of violence?"

"Call it an abundance of caution. But, yes, you do what you can to protect family."

I said, "I get that. I'm sure Amanda and Mark will enjoy the company, too. Can't you stay on the island?"

"I'll be back soon. Right now, they are shorthanded in people who can deliver the satphones and set up power stations. Once most key locations have re-established communication with society, I should be able to get away and come back."

I thought about what Steve said about the need for an active line of communication. "Steve, have we lost contact with the Nest?"

"We have. I went with Mark and Jerry to the shallow meeting site, and Charlie was out looking for us. We had a brief interaction, and I tried to convey that the tablets were broken, but we couldn't exchange any information without translation equipment. So, Charlie knows we are present on the island. I'm sure he and the Elders are confused."

"Did the EMP take out the underwater communication stations?" I asked.

"The shallow water site is down. We haven't been able to do a dive to check the equipment on the reef slope."

Peter asked, "Why not?"

"We don't have an operational boat to take to the reef slope. Even if I go out with the sailboat, we don't have a compressor for dive tanks. It's just too risky."

"Steve, this is Samantha again. I understand that people come first. But, for the same reasons that people need your satellite phones, we need to re-establish communication with the Nest. Our alliance is still new and fragile. I think we need to make sure we allocate resources to getting translation equipment in place."

"We're on the same page, Sam. That's why I went out on the reef with Mark and Jerry. I didn't want Jerry deciding to walk out to the reef edge with a tank and go down on his own. It didn't go well when you did that."

I was silent and felt a burn of blush on my face. *Was everyone looking at me?*

"Yeah, we don't want that," I said. "Do you have one of the computer-integrated phones that you gave us to bring here? You know, a phone with a self-contained translation program?"

"No, the only working phones I have are the ones from Canada. All the high-tech ones from the Georgia Tech team were fried by the EMP blast. What are you thinking?"

"The original program was on the mainframe computer at Georgia Tech. Did we lose that as well?" Peter asked.

"I don't know. Well, I know all the computers were fried, but they must have storage for programs somewhere. It's likely as soon as they have operational computers, they can have the program up and running."

"Do you think they can bypass computers and install the program on one of the new phones you have from Canada?"

"You know, in all this confusion, I forgot you and Peter have had enhanced phones. Are you using them to run the avatar program?"

"We are," I said. "It took a while for the local octopuses to accept the use of the avatar, but it's working now."

"We've been working on the translation software and building a local dictionary. We would need to restore the Nest language to a phone."

Peter said, "It's a good thing we have two phones."

There was silence in the room.

"Steve, are you still there?"

He asked, "Could you control the avatar from your site, using your phone?"

The idea was tempting, but with so many linked technologies, I had doubts. "I don't know. You need to ask the computer guys if it could work."

Steve said, "Don't get too excited. I'm not sure these phones are good enough for the capacity you'll need, and even if they are, I don't know when the Georgia Tech people will retrieve programs from storage tapes. But I'll check with our computer and electronics team."

Chapter 48 ~Blue~New Friends?

Heron Reef, Australia

The humans were giving more information now. The meetings have expanded from the exchange of names for creatures to a fascinating sharing of ideas about the world.

I should say, about our two worlds, for we were creatures of the sea and reef, and the humans live above the surface, in a world we knew very little about. It seemed that humans knew a great deal about our world and have been exploring it for some time. They had machines that permitted them to come to the reef and stay underwater. We visited the shallow tide pools and glimpsed the world of the surface but could not truly grasp the world of air.

So we had many questions, and we asked them. But many answers seemed slippery and difficult to understand. Like, movement. We asked how humans move when they were in their worlds. Samantha spoke of walking on legs. We understood walking. We did that too. She spoke of running to move fast. And I think I understand running. Then I asked about moving very fast, like when we jet to get away from a predator or pulse to move through the water above the surface.

Samantha messaged about flying in an airplane. Her message seemed like nonsense, and I told her so. She showed images on the display mat. I asked if these were creatures like the great whales of the ocean. But she said they were not alive.

I was not certain of the word *alive*. Was she saying the airplane was like a whale that had died? Samantha described the size of an airplane, and it sounded like a whale. How could such a large structure never have been alive? How could such a large thing move through the air like a whale moved through water?

Food should be simple. There was joy in seeing a fish or crab and skillfully capturing food for yourself or for the young. Humans are things they didn't capture. We understood plants. We sometimes ate the algae off rocks, mostly when hunting was poor, but sometimes for taste. Samantha said humans made algae grow and then captured it to eat. She said they made creatures grow too.

When Samantha talked about making creatures grow for food, our meeting ended. Gray and the others found the ideas disturbing and questioned Samantha for details. After a short time, we left the meeting, agreeing to explore the topic at a future meeting. Truly, we must not understand the words. How could one creature make another grow?

Gray asked about human Younglings, asking how humans reproduce and who raised the young. Samantha said that a male and female raised one Youngling at a time but was not able to explain how eggs are fertilized. We might need more words.

After returning to our Nest, Gray and I talked about the meeting and the difficulty of understanding creatures so different from us. We agreed that Samantha was wise in starting our meetings by building a shared vocabulary. That was simple. We needed to try to find simple questions to ask—ones that we have more ability to understand.

With such strange creatures who were so different from us, how would one find a simple question?

Chapter 49 ~ Samantha ~ Small World

Heron Island, Australia

The Georgia Tech team had Peter reset his phone to a previous backup, pointing out that they didn't have access to the cloud, but we did. It was brilliant. Now my phone had the dictionary we were building to communicate with Blue, and Peter's was restored to the program he had before the Australia trip. So, his phone now had language to talk to the Nest.

"Well, we took care of what we could. I don't know what else we can do from here," Peter said.

"It's frustrating being halfway around the world when there is a crisis at home. I feel so helpless," I said.

"Yeah," Peter said, then looked at me, tilting his head.

"What?" I asked.

"You have that look on your face. If you have an idea, share it."

"You remember that solar-powered sailing vessel that joined us in Cuba?" I asked.

"Sure."

"I wonder where it is now. It had a sophisticated satellite communication system on board."

"They were from Australia. It's unlikely they are still in North America," he said.

"I know, we can look into them, but the idea is to find a vessel in the Caribbean, outside of the EMP blast zone, with satellite communication ability and have them travel to Georgia."

We were sitting in the mess hall over dinner. Sally and everyone but Peter were staring at me like I was nuts.

"What's wrong?" I asked. "It's a reasonable suggestion."

"Samantha, I don't want to bust your bubble, but I don't think there are a lot of yachts outfitted with the equipment you guys will need hanging around the Caribbean. And if you find one, it's unlikely they will take it into hostile territory—basically a war zone."

"Well, if I don't look, I can't find one."

Peter hadn't said anything, but he was nodding, and I figured he knew what I had in mind.

He said, "You're going to post on the academic websites where you first released Charlie's video, right?"

"I am. We need to find someone already interested in the project, who knows what we are doing, and will help."

Sally added, "Who also has a sophisticated communication system on a boat close enough to Georgia to make the trip."

"Yeah. And it can't be Cuba. The EMP blast took them out," Peter added.

I said, "It's a shame. You know they would help if they could."

Peter said, "You're onto something. Compose a message spelling out what we are trying to do and what we need. People in blackout zones won't even see it. People who are too far away will either not respond or say they wish us luck but can't help."

"It can't hurt. We might even find colleagues from Cuba, who are in another part of the Caribbean, outside the EMP blasts and in a position to help."

"Okay. What equipment do we need? Help me plan the posting. "

An hour later, I had what I needed for a campaign: locate a high-tech, rich, octopus-loving volunteer. How hard could it be?

Peter suggested we use Jerry's initial video of me, as a fourteen-year-old, interacting with Charlie as a hook and follow with a video showing a display mat used for conferencing. He had the videos on his phone, and they automatically downloaded when he restored it. That was so sweet that he had them. I didn't carry them around!

Then, I gave an update on the work on treating bleached coral and how the octopuses of the Nest were partnering with us. We included a video of two Brothers carrying a probiotic and using a syringe to treat corals. Finally, I pitched the need to re-establish communication and the equipment we needed in Georgia to make it happen.

I posted the request at nine at night before going to bed. By the morning, I had an avalanche of messages. Most wished us good luck and expressed regret that they could not offer help. But, as I worked through message after message, I found it—or, at least, I thought it was possible.

***

His name was Dick Finley, and he wasn't a scientist. Dick was a retired business executive, an avid sport diver, and a competitive spear fisherman. I wondered how he came across the posting. He told me he found the link on popular diving forums. Someone had thought to repost the link on nonacademic sites. I would be forever grateful to whoever thought to do that.

Dick and his diving buddies were on his yacht in Jamaica. They didn't want to return home until power was re-established. But he loved octopuses, and he had the communication equipment we needed.

Chapter 50~ Samantha ~ S.A.M. reaches out

This meeting would be a first in so many, many ways that I was having trouble focusing on what to do. We had talked about communicating with the Nest from a "dry" site but had never tried to implement the process. Now, I would be trying to communicate with Charlie from a dry site halfway across the world. *Would the time lag be manageable?*

Dick's vessel was at Coastal Eleven, and he had a gimbal-mounted parabolic satellite dish on the deck of the yacht. Once the boat was in position, anchored off the reef crest of Coastal Eleven, they would run a fiber cable from the satellite dish controller down to the deep-water communication site on the sea floor at a depth of ten meters. The yacht had a state-of-the-art computer linked to the satellite dish to prepare the information for transmission to the geosynchronous satellite. Dick liked his toys and never wanted to be without the ability to communicate should he run into mechanical issues, bad weather, or people not on good behavior. He was an adventurer at heart but not foolhardy.

Our part of it was simple. Well, it was relatively simple. We cleared a space on the floor of the research lab and positioned the display mat in a shallow tank. We tried using the display mat dry, but the avatar didn't have the right optics without at least half a meter of water over the display mat. It took a minimum of half a meter of water for the avatar to look right. While we didn't actually need to see the avatar on this end, I lacked confidence. I wanted to see that S.A.M. was doing what I programmed him to do. We had a display monitor on the wall to show the Runt and Charlie. Jerry would have a camera on them, linked to the dish on the yacht's deck.

If it all worked, we would see Charlie and Runt as they responded, and the images would feed into Peter's phone for translation. We would hear their "words" on the phone speaker. Just thinking about the sequence of steps made my head spin.

***

Dick was a jovial man in his mid-to-late forties. He was fit and well-tanned from excessive time in the sun, with a bald head by choice. He avoided the gray receding hairline by shaving his head. The overall effect was striking. He looked like he would feel at home on the set of an action film.

Having sailed five days to bring *The Esmeralda* from Jamaica to Coastal Eleven, Dick felt entitled to request a spot on the dive team, and Mark wasn't inclined to argue with him once he was confident Dick's diving buddy could operate the elaborate telecommunication equipment. Dick promised to observe and to stay out of the way.

Jerry stood on the deck holding a camera, half a dozen pieces of equipment, and a roll of fiber cable.

"Are you all set?" Mark asked.

Jerry said, "I hope so. The camera isn't too different. The idea of working tethered by a fiber cable makes it intimidating."

"I'm sure you'll do fine. Remember, you're not filming a documentary. Keep the camera angle and distance as constant as possible without zooming in or pulling back for effect."

"I figured that. We need clear imaging for translation. I get it. No artistic stuff."

"The big question is if will they show up?" Mark said.

"I know," Jerry said. "Watching Dr. Kelly tell Charlie about this meeting was like watching a game of pantomime."

"Well, let's go down and see."

Chapter 51: Charlie~Old Friends

Coastal Eleven Reef, Georgia

The Elder Counsel was skeptical when I said the humans wanted to meet at the deep site. Maybe I wasn't convincing, because I wasn't sure I understood Jerry correctly. Without human technology, I was guessing at much of what they messaged. But they agreed that Runt, Archimedes, and I would wait at the site.

We came to the deep site at high tide and waited where we had met with the humans countless times. It was a space resting between two long coral buttresses at the base of the reef wall, with a large stretch of sand perfect for humans to place the communication mat. The site was also open and large predators were common, so we stayed hidden along the wall, nestled in the branching coral, waiting and watching as fish swam by.

We had visited this site many times looking for our missing humans, pressing the signal to ask for a meeting, but no one came. I wished I were *sure* of Jerry's meaning. His use of coral rubble was like Samantha's before we used the tablets and display mats.

"How long will we wait?" Archimedes signaled.

"You do not need to wait with us," I answered.

"Yes. How long will you wait?" he repeated.

"We will wait until the light dims. Mark and Jerry never come to the reef

in the dark."

Archimedes messaged, *"I will wait with you."*

We waited, and I wondered if they would come if I had understood Jerry and Mark's positioning of coral. I was almost ready to leave when the shadow of the boat moved across the reef and stopped a distance from us. The shadow was large, and the boat anchored a distance from us. I thought they must need even deeper water. We watched four humans enter the water.

They were all male. Three stayed as a tight group, and one followed from behind.

"I recognize Jerry and Mark, but not the other two," messaged Archimedes and Runt.

"I think the human making many bubbles might be the Elder that came to the reef flat with Jerry and Mark," Runt responded.

I looked again. Runt might be right. Samantha said that many bubbles were a sign a diver was nervous and inexperienced or someone who hadn't used diving equipment for a long time. This human would run out of air before the others.

The fourth human, trailing behind stayed a distance from us and set up camera equipment. None of us recognized this human. It might have been his first time with us at the meeting site.

We moved from our shelter to the display mat and waited for the humans to bring a phone or tablet to the mat. I watched as Mark rolled a mat onto the sand. A cord snaked its way from the mat upward through the water rising to the boat. The cord was new. *Was this how the humans would make the technology work again?*

Jerry started the program, and one mat showed a still image of S.A.M., the octopus avatar we used when we communicated with the Cuban Nest. But this image was still. Maybe the humans were still trying to get the technology working.

"Why is the avatar still?" I messaged Mark.

But the image remained still.

Archimedes messaged, *"Why did they have us meet here when they still can't communicate?"*

I messaged back, *"Give them time. They wouldn't have asked us here without good reason."*

We waited a long time. Then, the avatar composed a message, "Hi Charlie, This is Samantha."

I messaged, *"Samantha? Are you not in Australia?"*

The avatar messaged, "I'm controlling the avatar from very far away because the devices at Coastal Eleven are not working. They asked me to operate the avatar and explain what happened. They wanted the Nest to understand why Mark and Jerry were not at the meeting site. Charlie, because I am far away, there will be a lag between when you message, and I see your message. It will take a long time for you to get my answer. Be patient."

I messaged, *"Why do Jerry and Mark not have working tablets? What has happened?"*

It took a long, long time before S.A.M. the avatar began to move again. I was glad that Samantha had warned me to be patient.

The avatar delivered a complicated message. "The humans at Coastal Eleven have suffered widespread technology failures. They are working to repair and build new devices, but now, boat travel and communication tablets are not working. The boat they used for this meeting came from an island near Cuba."

I paused to consider who I should answer. I was not communicating with Mark. The message came from Samantha in Australia.

I faced the mat and delivered my message to the still avatar. *"Saman-tha, my friend. It is good to communicate with you through the avatar. It is confusing to think we can communicate with you in Australia, but not with Mark and Jerry, who are right here. So I ask you, how were so many human machines are affected at once?"*

"Charlie, this was the action of bad humans and was done deliberately. When the equipment is repaired and Mark can continue your lessons, you will learn about actions like these."

I messaged, *"How long before the machines can be repaired?"*

"I do not know exactly how long. I will continue to communicate using the avatar to keep you aware of the progress."

I flashed a sequence of blue and green, showing I understood. *"Samantha, I know Mark and Jerry. I think the diver breathing too quickly is the Elder who gave us the message to come today. Who is the fourth diver who stays by himself?"*

"His name is Dick Finley, and he owns the large boat. He is very interested in octopuses and asked to observe this meeting. His boat has the communication equipment that makes it possible for me to control the avatar."

"Please welcome him to the Nest, and say we thank him for bringing the team out to the site."

"I will convey the message. Charlie, it might be awhile before regular meetings can resume. We didn't want you to worry. The divers need to return to the boat now. When we can come back, Mark will leave a signal at the shallow site. He will leave smooth stones."

"We will check the site daily. When we see smooth stones, we will return to the deep site on the next high tide."

Chapter 52 ~Blue~Distant Relatives

Heron Reef, Australia

We moved from the shelter of corals out into the opening, where we had met with Samantha before. But there were now two mats where there had been one on the sand. We waited patiently while our visitors positioned the mats and set up other equipment. Humans seemed to use a lot of equipment.

Parrot fish swam between coral formations, darting in to graze on coral and giving rise to an ever-present clicking sound. We settled next to the communication equipment.

"Why are they using two mats?" Gray asked.

"Samantha said the second mat was for her friend Charlie to join our meeting."

"Charlie is an octopus?"

"Yes."

"How can he join the meeting using a mat?"

"That is unknown to me. We will soon see."

Peter operated the mat, and S.A.M.'s image appeared on the first mat. His tentacles moved as he composed a message. "Hello, thank you for agreeing to meet. We are excited to introduce you to a member of a distant Nest, Charlie."

The second display mat powered on, and an octopus appeared. Like the avatar, this octopus had the same coloration as S.A.M. But, the tentacle motion was fluid, like ours. This was no avatar.

"Can Charlie see us?" I asked.

"Charlie is on his reef in Georgia, looking at a display mat on the sand. He sees you as a moving image in the sand."

"How?" I asked. *"Can you explain how the humans make this happen?"*

"Technology is complicated, and we do not have all the words we would need. But in short, a camera device records images and motions. Other devices send the recorded scene over long distances. The image ends up on the display mat in front of Charlie and other members of the Nest."

"Is Charlie in front of the mat now?" I asked.

"He is," the avatar messaged. "Charlie will see your motions and colors when you compose a message. Your language is unique, and you will not understand Charlie's meaning—the human technology will translate, and then the avatar will repeat the message in your language.
"

I messaged the image, *"I am Blue, and I welcome you to our Nest."*

I watched the display. It was disturbing. Charlie's tentacle motions seemed familiar, and I felt I should understand, but none of his movements came together meaningfully.

As soon as Charlie ended his message with his tentacles coming to rest, the avatar began moving.

"It is great to see you and your Nest, knowing how far away you are. Human technology is impressive."

Then, the avatar was still. The message was complete.

I began again. *"We are learning many unfamiliar names and words from Samantha and Peter, but this is new. I understand you have been communicating with humans for a long time."*

As I watched Charlie, I noticed he moved small pieces of coral on the sand. It must be part of his language. Once again, as soon as he was still, the avatar started to message.

"I was a Youngling on my first exploration when I met Samantha. That was our first communication with humans. It feels like a long time, but our meetings with humans have all been within my lifetime."

I asked, *"Why do the humans want to talk to you or us?"*

Charlie took a while before starting his reply. His message was beautiful to watch when he did even though his movements did not convey meaning to me. It was a long and complicated message, and I was glad to see it first from Charlie before viewing the avatar's translation. There was emotion in Charlie's movements. I saw joy, wonder, warmth, and affection. Then he was still, and the avatar gave meaning to his motion.

"I was a young explorer, and I found in Samantha a kindred spirit—she, too, was an explorer on the reef. As we became friends, I learned about humans. There are many human explorers. The discovery of unknown places and new life is valued. There was much excitement in the human Nest when they learned of marine life capable of communication. At first, this drove them to work with me and develop a shared vocabulary. Then we found we could be partners and friends. We care for corals and tend to the coral reef."

The avatar was a wonder. I could understand the message's meaning but watching confirmed my first impression. The avata lacked the subtle motions that give emotion to our language. S.A.M. came across as cold and unfeeling. It was good that I could watch Charlie as well.

Chapter 53~Alana~Rotation

Coastal Eleven, Georgia Barrier Island.

Restoring power to local communities was frustratingly slow. The problem wasn't a lack of computer chips and equipment. Components from Canada made their way into the affected states every day. With a growing number of restored power stations and strategic placement of portable solar charging units positioned strategically along the eastern coastline, a small fleet of electric vans ferried the needed supplies. Now, it was the lack of technicians and engineers needed for repairs that left people in the dark.

Still, tensions eased when power stations flickered to life one by one. News of the restorations spread to neighboring towns, and people hungry for hope accepted that while progress came in bursts, there would be a return to "normal." The reopening of grocery stores brought a shift in outlook. Even though the stores operated under military supervision with people using government-issued ration cards, shopping felt comforting. People became impatient rather than panicked. Fear of violence and looting faded.

Life at Coastal Eleven settled into a comfortable new pattern. Dick Finley kept his yacht at the island, providing transportation for Mark and Jerry to the reef meetings with the Nest. He also made regular runs to the mainland for food and other supplies and to transfer personnel.

Dick's background was in business, but his passion was scuba diving. The communication with octopuses filled him with awe. Dr. Kelly offered him a position in NOAA as a boat captain. Now the island had an additional cottage, although most nights, Dick slept on *The Esmeralda*.

This morning, *The Esmeralda* journeyed to New Savanah for a personnel rotation. Jerry needed to return to Georgia State, which had reopened and encouraged students to return. Alana had been relieved of her duties at the mainland NOAA research facilities and would stay at Coastal Eleven, stepping into Jerry's duties.

From shore, Alana watched *The Esmeralda* pull into the harbor. Jerry stepped onto the dock and secured a mooring line. She had been at the port waiting for over an hour and was dismayed at the desolate atmosphere of the once-thriving coastal town. After the EMP blast, the local businesses closed. After three months, the fishing and ferry companies, still waiting for replacement electrical engine parts, were docked and unmanned. Empty shops and eateries contributed to a ghost-town atmosphere.

Jerry was taller and well-muscled. He wasn't the out-of-shape, somewhat overweight pre-teen she remembered from when they first met. "Jerry, it's been a while. I think you grew another inch or two."

Jerry gave her an affectionate hug. "Maybe, I don't know the last time I checked my height. I don't even know how tall I am now. You ready for island life?"

"Absolutely. I love living at Coastal Eleven. I'm particularly excited about the conferences with Blue."

"Do you think he'll remember you from when you were at Heron?" Jerry asked.

"Maybe, but I only met Blue a few times. How about you? Are you ready for life back at Georgia State?"

"I'm nervous. I haven't been in a city since the EMP. Dr. Kelly says things are settling down, but I should stay on campus and around people, not wander off. Still, uneasy or not, I need to get back to my classes."

"I've been on campus a few times in the last two weeks. It feels reasonably normal. They even have the cafeteria up and running," Alana said.

"Really? What about rationing?"

"Yeah, the ration. It looks like the cafeteria is 'normal,' but the school restricts selections to match a ration-based meal. Breakfast is oatmeal, lunch is bean and vegetable soup and rolls with a small serving of cheese. At dinner, it's rice with a stir fry."

"I guess you show ration cards to get in?" Jerry said.

"Yes. Did Dr. Kelly suggest you not go anywhere alone?" Alana asked.

"Yeah. Is it that bad?"

"Things can still feel a bit mixed. Campus is safe, but make sure you're not the last to leave at night. There are the usual police, but they've pulled the National Guard now, and there are still muggings. The buzz phrase is *maintain situational awareness*."

"It's not like we carry money anymore. What do muggers take?"

"A friend of mine got mugged last week, and they took his shoes. Bill said the guy was almost apologetic but needed the shoes."

"Wow."

"I'll admit, I'm looking forward to being at Coastal Eleven. I'm assuming I don't have to worry about being mugged."

"Not likely."

Dick finished tying *The Esmeralda* to the dock and walked over to join them. He extended his hand and said, "You must be Alana."

"Yes, welcome to the team. Dr. Kelly told me how you stepped in to help to save the day. He's quite grateful."

"This has been the most exciting thing to happen ever. The project is incredible. I hear you're the researcher that pointed them toward Blue's Nest."

"Yes, and I hated leaving so soon after the discovery. I'm looking forward to taking part in the meeting."

Dick said, "Alana, make yourself comfortable onboard. I need to check in with the harbormaster and pick up supplies. Jerry, I'll see you next time. Enjoy being back in civilization."

Jerry asked, "Do you need me to help load your supplies?"

Alana said, "Jerry, you need to catch the train. It's not like the old days. Only one train runs every other day. You have forty-five minutes, but you should head to the station." Alana flexed her muscles in a mock He-Man pose. "I'll help Dick load the crates. We'll be fine."

Jerry headed to the train station, aware that once Alana and Dick were out of sight, he was indeed alone. They hadn't restored the trolley yet, so he adopted a brisk pace for the five blocks to the train station.

Chapter 54 ~ Jerry ~New Normal

Georgia State University, Atlanta Georgia

Jerry closed the door to the dorm and tossed his bag on the bed. Few students had returned to campus, and the emptiness gave the lie to any expectation that life had returned to "normal." The gray dorm walls seemed dreary. Samantha used to bring pictures to brighten the room. For once, Jerry wished he had brought pictures of Coastal Eleven to hang. He always considered that a girl thing, but now he was reconsidering.

In normal times, Jerry rarely spent much time in the dorm. His coursework often included film projects, and he was either out on a shoot or in the lab processing the video recordings. He studied in the library for academics, and his science classes had hands-on laboratory activities that kept him busy for most of his evenings.

Georgia State had enough students with hybrid online classes, and the science labs were almost all open, so students could come in and do a lab when they were on campus. But these were not "normal times." The city and campus were slowly coming back to life. However, transportation issues and food shortages persisted, and there were distressing instances of looting and violence. Georgia State offered online access to all classes because many students were nervous about returning. Some feared being in the city. Others were nervous about leaving older parents to cope with the social chaos at home.

Returning the Georgia State campus to its previous bustling and thriving academic environment would take time. For now, classes were less than 50 percent full, and the dorms remained depressingly empty. The impact of the EMP blast hovered everywhere, from a lack of air conditioning to constant internet failures, but most of all, in the empty nature of the campus. Jerry wondered if he had made a bad choice coming back this early. Mom pushed him to go, saying she wanted him to continue his program and that things were stable at Coastal Eleven. It still felt wrong. He was sitting on his bed when he heard the door to the quad open.

"Hey Jerry, you're back!" Pete said, poking his head into Jerry's room.

Relief swept over him, and he flashed a genuine smile. "Yeah, I'm back. Good to see you."

Pete Gallagher was one of the four students in Jerry's dorm quad, and the only one he liked. The others were "dating." Jerry didn't care for their girlfriends, who seemed to be at college solely to find husbands. He talked about them at home, and his mom and Samantha were incredulous that any female students still had that mindset. Then Amanda pointed out that admission policies at Georgia State were more flexible than at Georgia Tech, and there would be girls who graduated from high school in Atlanta and went to the local college because it was convenient.

"When did you get in?" Jerry asked.

"Last Wednesday. My dad had business in Atlanta, so we took the train together. He left yesterday after helping me settle in."

Jerry said, "It's amazing that we can take it for granted the train is running. It seemed like we were in meltdown mode just yesterday, wondering what happened and if the crises would ever end."

"I'll say. Now, I just get annoyed when the server is down, and I can't get online or when I reach for my nonexistent cell phone. God, I miss cell phones."

Jerry pointed to the box sitting on his desk. "My supervisor supplied one and told me to protect it against another attack. The box is a Faraday case. It isolates electronics and protects against an EMP blast."

Pete stared at Jerry's desk. He looked at the cell phone then back at Jerry, his face a composite of shock and envy. "How do you have a working cell phone? I thought the blast fried all the towers?"

"It's my work satellite phone. It doesn't use a cell phone tower. Of course, I can only use it to talk to people who have satellite service or people outside of the blast area who have cell service."

"The box is a Faraday device?" Pete asked, looking skeptical.

"It is. The sides, top and bottom, have a fine mesh of metal embedded in the fabric lining the wood. I can't carry the phone around like a regular cell phone."

"Can I see the phone?" Pete asked.

Jerry hopped off his bed and went to the desk. He opened the neat black box, showing what looked like an older cell phone. It was considerably larger than a normal phone with an old-fashioned small screen and actual keyboard buttons built in. The box also contained a small tablet.

"The tablet is nothing special, except they shipped it from Canada after the blast. I can use the satellite phone as a connection point for the tablet when the campus internet is down."

"I see you keep both in the box. Are you expecting another attack?"

"I hope not. But my boss wants me to be cautious with the equipment and keep it in the box when I'm not using it. He said we would all feel foolish if we had it unprotected and another attack left us just as cut off and helpless as the first one. We can't pretend it couldn't happen. We know it can."

Pete nodded in agreement. "I just wish we knew who did it and why."

"Me too," Jerry said. "Me too."

Chapter 55~ Charlie ~Silent Conversation

Coastal Eleven Reef, Georgia Barrier Island

I reached a tentacle and manipulated the switch to activate the display mat and camera. In front of me, a still avatar came into view. The camera was mounted and focused on a square platform marked on the sand. As long as I stayed within the boundaries, the computer system would capture my movements and color sequences. The translation program would direct the avatar to deliver my message to the Nest in Australia. My brains hurt thinking about the human technology we used.

Blue in Australia controlled the avatar before me. I would see motions and color sequences translated so that we could understand Blue's message.

Samantha told me to ignore the camera and suggested that I "talk" to the avatar, treating it like a visiting octopus, an equal. She and warned us of a time delay because of the vast distance between us. Mark suggested we treat the avatar as a "slow-responding visitor."

Today would be our fifth meeting with the Australian octopus Nest, but the first one using the automated system without humans mediating and operating the avatars. Messaging through human-operated avatars was awkward.

The presence of humans was distracting, making it hard to concentrate on what the cyanea were messaging. We hoped that the new system would lead to more natural interactions.

I was not sure I could succeed at ignoring technology, but I would do my best. Archimedes helped me compose a greeting, and he, along with Runt and Learner, stayed nearby to observe.

So, I began the meeting by signaling to the still image and feeling foolish.

The avatar before us was pale blue, quite different from our S.A.M. avatar Samantha used to meet with us. Humans designed this avatar to mimic the appearance of the Australian octopuses.

I messaged, *"I greet you, Blue, and the Elders of your Nest."*

Then I waited, remembering Mark's warning that the avatar would respond slowly. The avatar blinked out of existence for a moment, then reappeared, moving and displaying a familiar sequence of colors.

Blue messaged, *"It is wondrous to think of reaching across the distance to meet others of our kind."*

I knew humans would record our interactions and analyze the information we exchanged. But without Mark and Jerry or Alana by my side, it was easy to forget about humans. Whenever a traveler from another Nest arrived, it was a big event. One or more members of the Elder Counsel attended these meetings. We were hungry for information from distant Nests. That was never more true than for today's meeting. I was on the Elder Counsel, but Archimedes watched from a distance. We would share information from this meeting with the entire Nest.

"Blue, how many Brothers and Elders are in your Nest?"

"We are a small colony, not a Nest. Our Nest is on a reef nearby, separated by a single day's journey. It is our way to send Brothers to explore."

"It is our way as well. On my first exploration as a Brother, I discovered the Coastal Eleven reef, where we made our Nest."

Blue asked, *"How many octopuses are in your Nest?"*

"It varies depending on how many eggs reach Youngling status. But our Nest is unusual. Many Brothers travel to our Nest and remain. They are interested in our communication with humans. Our Nest is larger, over a hundred Brothers."

Blues' colors showed surprise, and he messaged that none of their Nests reached those numbers.

The translation program adjusted Blue's message, presenting it in motions and color sequences we used. It wasn't long before I forgot about communicating through an avatar. Even the time delay faded into the background. It was fascinating that our Nests, so far apart in distance, were so alike.

The Australian octopuses had an Elder Counsel that assigned tasks to the Brothers. One thing of particular interest was that the Australian octopuses selected individuals for the honor of reproduction. The nonbreeding individuals had much longer lifespans and raised the Younglings. They had more in common with us than Nests of the Cuban octopuses.

It was a mystery. Why would these octopuses, who lived so far away, have so many traits the same as us?

Chapter 56 ~ Samantha~New Normal

Heron Island, Australia

"Peter, look at the tentacle speed on the video. Are we seeing the feed at high speed? Is something glitching?"

"I don't think so. The fish in the background are moving at a normal speed," Peter said.

The split screen displayed the octopuses from two Nests in a ballet of elegant movements with brilliant colors flashing across tentacles. Blue's Nest was a kilometer offshore here on Heron Reef. On the right of the display, Blue messaged with Gray behind him. Charlie, with Archimedes behind him, was on the left side of the display. Coastal Eleven was half a world away.

Using automated technology, octopus populations could "meet" without human moderation. We were witnessing a historic "first" in science.

Was this why they looked like they were messaging at warp speed?

I said, "I think they've been slowing down for us. Now that humans aren't part of the conversation, they can 'talk' at their normal speed."

Dr. Snyder said, "You mean they talk to us slowly like we do when someone doesn't speak English."

"That makes sense," I said.

The tentacle motions were faster than I'd ever seen in one of our meetings with the Nest. But once I realized the motions were the same ones I was familiar with, but faster, I picked up traces of what Charlie was saying. But not Blue. I wondered if I would pick up the local language before it was time for us to return to the States.

"So, the display mats at the sites show the avatars?" Dr. Kelly asked.

"Yes, Charlie is seeing Blue's avatar using the computer-provided translation. Blue is seeing the S.A.M. avatar using the local language," I said.

I adjusted the display settings to show the avatars and watched the four windows long enough to satisfy my curiosity. The avatars were moving just as fast as their living counterparts. We were the weak link, and with the humans no longer moderating the conversation, the avatars were only limited in speed by the processors of the translation computer—infinitely faster than we humans could type into keyboards. For the first time, we witnessed what octopuses looked like when they were deep in conversation and did not include us dumb humans. It made me realize just how stunted my communication with Charlie remained, even with all the progress through the years.

I switched the display back to the split screen, removing the avatars. Now, a written translation appeared as a line below each octopus. Because of the time lag, the translation was out of sync with the video feed—but we couldn't tell. It looked like close captioning or subtitles on a foreign film.

I glanced at the captioning enough to know they were comparing information on the organization of their colonies and the roles of Elders. I was glad they were recording everything so we could view it again at a more comfortable speed. Watching Charlie, I could almost follow what he was saying. Watching Blue made me realize how much of Charlie's language I had learned and how lost I was with the Australian octopuses.

If I could watch the video alongside the translation, it might help me learn this new language. But right now, the videos were so captivating that I didn't want to be distracted by reading the captions, so I did my best to ignore them.

"I'm going to bring us some snacks from the kitchen," Sally said. "Does anyone have any requests?"

Glancing at my watch, I saw that the meeting was now in its second hour, longer than any meeting we had attended. Our need to return to the surface when we ran low on air limited the length of a meeting. It would be interesting to see how long the octopuses would continue exchanging information, no longer limited by our need to breathe.

"Thanks, Sally, anything easy will be fine," I said.

"You can tell me what I've missed when I return," she said.

"You can catch up by reading the transcript," I said.

Peter nudged me. "Sam, she was kidding. That was a joke."

Chapter 57 ~ Jerry~ Crises of Conscience

Georgia State, Atlanta

Life on Coastal Eleven settled into a comfortable pattern. Solar panels once again provided power for lights, cooking, and using modern devices, which were now upgraded against future EMP attacks.

Dick continued using *The Esmeralda* to ferry passengers and supplies to the mainland but now captained the pontoon boat to the reef meeting sites. Now that replacement parts for the electric motors put the more practical boat into use. Mark resumed his twice-a-week instructional meetings with Charlie and Runt. They suffered from limited connectivity to the outside world. But with satellite phones, they could talk to colleagues and friends on the mainland.

Jerry returned to campus when his academic administers made it known the classrooms and dorms had electricity and plumbing, and the Film Department equipment had been repaired and was operational. He was eager to work on editing his latest coral recovery documentary. There were shortages on campus. But a lack of ice cream and lack of food choices in the cafeteria were minor issues. Campus, like the island, was an oasis of "normal."

Jerry was unaware that conditions beyond the campus were not nearly as settled. Most houses in Atlanta were still lacked electricity. Service vehicles moved between neighborhoods, delivering safe water.

Sanitation services provided temporary portable toilets and wash stations. Police guarded food delivery vehicles that distributed rations to families.

Jerry didn't go into town often, but when he did, he noticed everyone seemed tired and run down. Their faces were drawn and lacked any sign of hope for better times. It made him uneasy about being on campus. He wondered if he could be doing more to help people and made an appointment to meet with the department chair to ask about differing his enrollment.

When he arrived, his adviser was at a desk covered with files. Jerry noticed his file open on top of the stack.

"Thank you for seeing me, Dr. Jordan."

"I'm always glad to meet with our students and pleased to welcome you back to campus. What can I help you with?"

"Sir, I'm thinking of putting my studies on hold. Considering current conditions, I could be doing more important work."

His supervisor put the file folder down.

"Are you saying your work promoting conservation efforts isn't important? Are you second-guessing your major?"

Jerry didn't say anything. He looked around the neat office, which seemed to hold the world's chaos at bay.

"Sir, when I walk off campus, I see houses without power and people waiting for government-supplied bottled water. It doesn't feel right to be working on something so, well, academic."

"Jerry, this is a university, and you *are* working on a college degree. So, the nature of things is academic. That doesn't mean unimportant."

"I know, and I will come back to it, but right now, I would feel better putting it on hold and working with the Red Cross as a volunteer. I saw that they were recruiting people to help distribute food and water. Can you approve a one-semester deferment?"

"I can, but you should think before doing that. You would need to pay back the tuition covered by your scholarship. Why not volunteer part-time?"

"I hadn't thought about the tuition."

"Jerry, I commend you for wanting to volunteer, and I know the Red Cross will be happy to have your help. But it's also important for the community to see signs that the world is returning to normal. Having the university in place, students with students, helps the world return to normal."

Jerry shifted and rubbed his hands, trying not to clench them. He hadn't considered the tuition. It was a lot of money.

"Let me talk to the local Red Cross branch about volunteering part-time. I want to continue my program. Although it feels like I'm hiding out on campus while people outside hang on by a thread."

"You're not hiding out. You're doing important work. Jerry, you were passionate about your documentaries and influencing public opinion."

"I'm still passionate about it. But I wonder if it's the most important thing I can be doing right now."

"I understand, and I applaud your sense of duty. Understand that, as a society, our future will be shaped by how we educate our young people so they can contribute to the world. Your studies are important, and you are already doing work that moves us in important ways. I can arrange a deferment if it's what you feel you must do, but I suggest you find a balance between volunteering and your studies. I see you are registered for a very heavy term. You could drop two classes and still be full time.

"Thank you. You've given me things to think about."

Jerry stood to leave, and Dr. Davis shook his hand. The world wasn't simple, but he would find his way through the difficult times.

Chapter 58 ~Charlie~ Lessons

Coastal Eleven Reef, Georgia Barrier Island

Mark tried to restart lessons on human culture and government as if nothing had happened. Runt and I stopped him and asked for information on the equipment failure and loss of communication. We could not understand much of his answer. There were many words and concepts that we could not process. It seemed that many of the failures involved electricity.

"Can you explain electricity again?" I asked.

Mark released many bubbles, startling the parrot fish, who quickly swam away. It took a while before he began to message.

"Electricity is like moving water. Think of powerful moving water that damages the reef during a storm."

"Yes, we understand that moving water breaks branches of coral during a storm," I said.

"Moving water has energy. That is why it breaks coral. Above the water, we have other forces that have energy. We have something called lightning. It is like sunlight but has more energy and can do more damage. Lightning travels through the air quickly. If it hits a human, the human will die."

"Does lightning move in water?" I asked. *"I do not think we know of a light that kills."*

"Lightning forms high in the atmosphere and travels quickly to the land or water. I don't know if it travels in the ocean."

"Did lightning cause your technology to fail?" I asked.

"No. I'm talking about lightning, so you might understand electricity."

"Is lightning electricity?" I asked.

"No. Let me try again. The light you use in communication is harmless, like the gentle movement of water. Electricity can be gentle. It has power but doesn't need to be destructive. Like water, it flows and powers much of human technology."

"This is so confusing," Runt messaged.

"I know," I replied.

"We might not understand electricity, but we understand that humans use electricity. Can you explain why your technology failed?" I messaged.

Mark paused, and I watched as he checked his air gauge. We had been down a long time, and the meeting would need to end soon. I hoped we would have some answers. Mark returned to his station and began to type his message.

"Charlie, you know that some humans are bad, like the ones that kidnapped you."

"Yes, and like the ones that kidnapped Samantha. I understand bad humans."

"The communication technology stopped working because bad humans used a kind of electricity like a giant wave to break human technology. It was like a water wave breaking coral. The 'wave' was an electromagnetic pulse called an EMP. This 'wave' broke technology that uses electricity."

"Did you catch the bad humans?"

"Not yet. We are looking and putting safeguards in place to protect against future use of an EMP."

"I am not sure I understand the actions of 'bad' humans. We do not have

Brothers who act against the good of the Nest. It has never happened."

"I am not sure I understand the actions of bad humans either. We do not know who used an EMP or why. It is troubling to all of us."

Runt messaged, *"From our studies, we know about countries and war. Was this an act of war?"*

"It could be. That is what we thought at first. But, it is possible that human 'Younglings' were trying to make a name for themselves as computer hackers."

"I do not understand."

"Younglings sometimes try to show their skill with computers by acts that disrupt computer systems. They might not have expected to be so successful. They might not have realized how much damage the EMP blast would cause."

"A Youngling would be able to do this?" I asked.

"Some Younglings are brilliant," Mark said.

"I would think discovering who used an EMP would be a top priority."

"It is a high priority. Our officials are working hard to find answers. But in the meantime, they are also working at preventing future attacks."

"I hope it is not one of your wars," I said.

"We don't think we are at war. If it were an attack by another government, there would have been additional acts against the United States. We will talk more of this, but we need to return to the surface," Mark said.

Mark and Alana rose in the water and disappeared from view.

I found the meeting frustrating and frightening. I didn't think I wanted to understand war. And the idea of human Younglings hacking to show how smart they were was maybe even more frightening. Humans were strange. The Elder Counsel would not be happy with our incomplete understanding of the event.

But, I was certain the humans were even more unhappy with their lack of answers.

Chapter 59 ~Samantha~Touching Base

Heron Island, Australia

I sat on the beach, watching eagle rays with their wings slicing through the water's surface. I couldn't remember when I last relaxed and enjoyed being on the beach. A jewel-colored sea stretched to the horizon, and the sounds of birds resonated like musical notes. Peter stood knee-deep in the water and watched tropical fish emerge from the rocks, occasionally nipping at his toes. We'd spent most of our time in Australia here at Heron, and I'd grown used to the island.

The excellent satellite signal strength at the island's far tip made the location ideal for what had been weekly phone calls with Mom. Now that they had a new satellite phone, we were trying to get back to our old pattern. So, this was Thursday morning, and Peter and I brought our coffee and took an early morning beach walk so I could have a visit. (Seven am Thursday on Heron was five pm in Georgia). It felt good not to be terrified of what was happening back home. All the recent news had been good. Even so, I got a little nervous before our weekly chats. The phone gave a beep.

"Peter, phone!" I called and waved. The caller ID said *Coastal Eleven*.

He nodded and walked up to join me.

"Hello, Mom?" I said.

"Sam. It's so good to hear your voice."

"I'm here too," Peter said.

"Hi Peter, have you two had a good week?"

"We have. It's an exciting time with meetings between the octopus Nests," Peter said.

I said, "I want to embrace being on this amazing island, but I also miss Coastal Eleven. And, with all that's happened at home, I wish I were there."

She said, "I can understand how you feel, and I won't lie. There are lots of times I wish you were here. But we're doing fine, and I want you to make the most of the opportunity to be part of an international community."

Hearing Mom's voice tightened my chest. Family dynamics could be complicated. When I was a kid, Dad was always the one I ran to and counted on for support. We were very close. Maybe it was because I was a science nerd, even as a kid, and he nourished my inner geek. Maybe it was because, like Dad, my skin was dark. I didn't know, but as a kid, I loved Mom, but we weren't close.

That changed after Dad died. Then, it was just Mom, Jerry, and me on the island. We counted on each other, and Mom helped me navigate through my wild teenage years and into adulthood. I couldn't have a kinder, more supportive adult than Mom. I was half a world away, and I missed her.

"I miss you too, Mom. Tell me what's happening at Coastal Eleven."

"Jerry left for Atlanta. We have the pontoon boat working again, and Alana works the camera for Mark when he meets with the Nest."

"I'm glad Jerry felt he could return to campus. How are the conditions in Atlanta?" I asked.

"Atlanta is still rough, but he tells me campus is safe and comfortable."

I said, "Tell him to stay on campus where it's safe."

"He wants to volunteer with the Red Cross."

"Of course he does," Peter said.

"I'm proud of him," Mom said. "But I'd rather have him safe. Post-EMP blast, everyone is stressed. Sam, I've spent too much time worrying about my kids. I deserve a break from worry, but it doesn't look like I'll get one."

Mom's anxiety was my fault. I was a difficult child. When I was twelve, I would head off from shore and spend hours exploring the reef flat alone. She never knew where I was. At fourteen, I took a skiff off the reef edge to stop Pharm Ex from collecting octopuses from the reef. The Coast Guard brought me back to shore when my skiff nearly capsized. Then there was the time that I went diving on my own and needed to swim to shore at night. That time, everyone was out looking for me. I didn't even want to think about the kidnapping in Cuba. Yeah, Mom deserved a break from worry.

"Mom, you're right. You deserve a break from worry, and I'm sorry I've given you so many opportunities for sleepless nights. But I grew up and settled down, and you can stop worrying about me."

"Sam, you're calling from Australia. That's not settled down."

"Yes, it is," Peter said. "Australia is just a location. We're respectable researchers at the University of Queensland's research station."

Mom said, "You're right, but I still worry. Will you stay the full year or come home?"

I was glad we had talked this over last night, and I was ready with an answer. "Alana says the Trans-Pacific ships plan to resume service in two months, as long as there are no attacks. As soon as we can book passage, we'll be home."

"Good. Even with the state of this country, I'll feel better knowing you could get home if you wanted to do so."

"You are so right about that," Peter said.

"Mom, we need to get to the lab. The team will be waiting for us."

"Go be brilliant," Mom said. "We'll talk next week."

"By Mom, love you," I said, and we headed back to the interior of the Island. We had work to do.

Chapter 60~Jerry~ Atlanta

Georgia State, Atlanta

"Good morning," Monica said

Jerry nodded and managed to mumble a "Good Morning" reply.

Monica was a cute redhead with a cheerful disposition and abundant, bubbly energy. Jerry found himself tong-tied around her.

They boarded the trolley to the downtown Red Cross center, and Monica sat next to Jerry.

"Great weather today. I bet a ton of people show up in the park," she said.

He looked up at the blue sky and said, "It is nice out today. I almost feel guilty volunteering instead of working on my school projects."

"Not too guilty," Monica said. "It's going to get hot this afternoon."

Jerry nodded, trying to think of something witty to say. They'd worked together for a month, and he wanted to ask her out. *Maybe today*, he thought.

At the center, Jerry collected food and water supplies. He moved between the long tables with protein bars, fruit, powdered milk, MREs (Meal, Ready to Eat), and five-liter refillable water tanks. Monica gathered personal hygiene supplies and books.

They reconvened at the loading dock, where Tim waited with a vehicle that looked like an old-fashioned mail delivery cart. Tim drove, navigating the cart onto a wide path that accommodated pedestrians on the left and bikes and the occasional official cart on the right. (Top speed was forty km/hour).

The distribution site at Rodney Cook Park was in Vine City, one of the few remaining suburbs in Atlanta without electricity or safe drinking water.

Almost everyone living in the area regularly visited the popular community park. Families brought children to the playground and often picnicked under the shade trees or at the tables under the large shade structure. It was an ideal location for volunteers to meet with the public and distribute relief goods, making life less stressful.

The Red Cross started distributing food and water within a week of the EMP blast. Police arrived with the volunteer workers to ensure violence didn't mar the deliveries. As tensions eased, the Red Cross told the officials they didn't need an escort. People seemed unwilling to fight over MREs or toothpaste.

Monica's table drew the largest crowd. She had books available to "loan" out, using an honor system with no record keeping. Still, folks were eager to keep the entertainment flow available, and most youngsters held books to return as they joined the queue, looking for something new to read.

It was early summer.

The EMP blast took place in winter and affected areas along the eastern coast of the southern states. So, the lack of energy for heating homes caused discomfort, not death. It was fortunate that the affected areas didn't have the deadly low temperatures of the northeast coast.

With summer approaching, the population would suffer from heat. The fossil fuel ban came with a redesign of homes to maximize airflow and natural cooling. People used dehumidifiers, fans, and localized cooling units. Without electricity, these folks would suffer.

Jerry set up water tanks so people could fill containers. Most folks were good-natured about bringing a container and not taking more than they needed. Water was heavy, and rumors abounded that the water system would be running any day now. Jerry handed bags containing food for one person, enough for a day. People could ask for more than one bag, but none of the food was popular enough to tempt hoarding.

When business slowed, Jerry took a glass of water to Monica.

"You have quite a crowd today. What's popular with the kids?"

Monica smiled and rolled her eyes. "Zombie apocalypse novels."

"You're kidding!"

Monica said, "No, and it's not just the kids. The adults are asking for them, too."

"Wow, I didn't expect that."

She said, "I guess it makes sense. The current situation doesn't seem too bad if you're reading a book about characters in an apocalyptic ruin running from zombies."

"I guess so," he said but didn't look convinced.

"Thank you for volunteering."

At first, Jerry worried that going into the city would be scary or depressing. His fears were short-lived. The folks at the relief stations were friendly and appreciative, and the work filled his need to be doing something. He lost the sense of helplessness that had plagued him since the EMP attack.

"Jerry, can you work with the shelter team next Wednesday?" Tim asked.

Jerry was silent. *How had he forgotten that they were entering the storm season?*

"I have a morning class that's over at ten. I could be here by eleven."

"I'll schedule you for an afternoon shift—they start at noon. The shelter is in Midtown. If you need a ride, be here at 11:30. We'll have a shuttle to take volunteers to the site."

With a warm ocean, hurricanes were possible six months of the year. The first of the storms would arrive in May; they would become more frequent in June and July. The truly frightening storms were a product of September and October. If he was right, whatever storm was wandering around in the Atlantic shouldn't be a big one.

"How far out is the storm?" Jerry asked.

"It's just a depression, and it might not develop. But it's time we set up shelters for hurricane season."

Jerry said, "Well, I'm hoping for a quiet season. We could use a break from disasters."

"Nature doesn't care what disasters we bring on ourselves."

"Yeah, I guess not. And, while hurricanes are natural disasters, you could argue that the super-storms were also disasters we brought on ourselves."

Chapter 61~ Samantha ~Is it time?

When the meeting ended, there was silence. Watching Charlie and Blue "talking" left me feeling empty inside, and I had difficulty processing the meaning of what we had witnessed.

"That was interesting," Dr. Snyder said.

Peter took his earpiece out and stretched. "Was anybody able to follow the conversation after the first five minutes?" he asked.

"You made it to five minutes?" Sally said. "I was lost within the first thirty seconds."

I said, "I was able to follow through most of the meeting, but just bits and pieces. I could figure out the main topic, but not the details."

"What were they talking about?" Dr. Snyder asked.

"They started with a discussion on Nest organization and history. After the first ten minutes, they mostly talked about us," I said.

"So, was the experiment a success?" Dr. Snyder asked.

I looked around the room. Everyone had their attention on me. It felt mildly uncomfortable. "I think so. Yes, we facilitated communication between two geographically separated populations of octopuses. They displayed high levels of interest in sharing information."

"I agree," Dr. Snyder said. "What comes next?"

I looked at Peter, and he shrugged.

"I don't know what's next for our tentacled friends, but I'm sure there will be more meetings," I said.

I looked at Peter. He gave me a nod, so I continued, "For us, it's time for Peter and I to go home."

"When?" Sally asked.

I said, "Soon". With a nod to Dr. Snyder, I added, "Dr. Snyder let us know that the cross-Pacific ferry has resumed transport to the United States. He also offered us an early release from our contract. "

Dr. Snyder said, "We love having you here, and hope you will be back, but all of us understand how eager you are to be with your families right now."

Peter said, "Thank you," and added. "It's been an honor and privilege. It is to work with all of you. This team is amazing, and we do hope to be back."

I added, "The world is getting smaller again. If you need me to step in with communication, we've discovered telecommunication by avatar is effective. We do hate to leave, but Peter and I need to be home to help rebuild."

Sally said, "I understand. It's just I planned on you being here through February. I'm going to miss you!"

I would miss Sally too. We had grown close this year, and I might never see her again. The thought didn't make me happy. Australia was so far away. Would I ever be back here?

"Sally, if I can work out a visiting faculty position at Georgia Tech, would you be interested?"

Her face brightened, and then the smile faded. "I don't know," she said. "America is so far away."

Peter nodded. "We can tell you from personal experience. It is a long trip, and you will miss home. But, you will meet amazing people and build great connections.

Her smile returned, and she nodded again. "I really will think about it. See if it might be possible."

Chapter 62 ~ Epilogue

Coastal Eleven, Georgia, 2052

The gazebo was perfect for family and friend gatherings. The platform fit nicely between the leeward side of sand dunes and the entrance to the Coastal Eleven habitat. On Friday, the NOAA vessel delivered the lightweight, inexpensive 3-D produced materials. On Saturday, the boys assembled the platform, support beams, and roof.

"You have the fried chicken?" I asked.

Mom said, "I do. Are you going to eat any?"

"I am," I said. I'd made my peace with the lab grown "new chicken." It was Peter's favorite food, and our daughter Marti had a taste for it, too. So I had little choice in the matter. We headed out the kitchen door, Mom carrying a big container of "chicken," me with a basket of bread, a variety of cheese, cut vegetables, and fresh fruit. I wondered what Monica and Sue would be bringing.

The full-time population of the island hadn't changed. Amanda and Mark ran the station. Mom still collected the physical data, and Mark was the full-time field biologist and managed the meetings with the Nest. But Coastal Eleven had lots of visitors these days. Researchers who wanted to visit the nest, and those of us with close ties to the island, the reef, and octopus friends.

Peter and I visited often. Marti wasn't even three but she already loved the island. Jerry came often, and we tried to coordinate visits so we could see each other. He often brought Monica with him. They weren't married, but I thought it was just a matter of time.

Jerry and Monica bonded while working with the Red Cross in the post-EMP event. They did catch the terrorists, and as Dr. Baker suggested, they were three American hotshots trying to make a name for themselves. Well, they succeeded. But it didn't land them a cushy job like they hoped. It landed them a prison sentence of twenty years. That blackout was part of history now.

It was a good thing our guys finished the gazebo for this weekend. We had a lot of people to feed, and there was no way everyone would fit around the kitchen table. The Martel extended family alone was now seven: Amanda, Mark, Jerry, Monica, Peter, Marti, and myself. Steve and Sue had sailed over for the weekend, and Alana rounded our group to a nice even ten.

It was a wonderful reunion, and it was nice to have space to socialize.

"Samantha, there you are!" Alana called from the gazebo where she and Peter were visiting while Marti played with her toys in the sand on the side of the platform and built sand castles, an activity she would do for hours if allowed to do so. She had been sifting through sand and had a collection of small shells and pieces of coral stacked like pieces of treasure.

"Look at that castle!" I said, kissing her on her head. She beamed and looked so happy.

"I love that you named her after Martel, even if you shorten her name. She looks just like your dad, you know."

"I know," I said.

Peter said, "I warned her Martelle would get shortened when she said she wanted to name her after your dad, and I was right."

"It's fine. I see Dad every time I look at her," I said.

Peter looked over the dunes to the sparkling blue water beyond. "Your dad would love that he has a grandchild named after him, even if the female form of Martel is a bit funny."

"I'm Marti," she said.

I laughed and hugged her. "Yes, you are my Marti."

Peter said, "Well, we know what name she likes."

Alana said, "You father was passionate about his work with climate change mitigation. Peter, he would love that Martel was named after him, but he would love more that you two felt confident enough about the future to have a child."

"I won't lie," I said. "I'm still concerned."

"We would have to be nuts to not be concerned," Peter said. "But life goes on, and looking at what we've accomplished, I think we are going to be alright."

Steve put his hand on my shoulder, and I almost jumped out of my skin. I hadn't heard him walk up.

"Steve, you scared me!" I said.

Steve said, "Sorry. Sam, I was listening in. I knew Martel very well. What he would be most proud of would be your work with the Nest. He bought the world time with his work on bioengineered coral seeding and reef expansion. You bought us more time by opening communication with the Nest."

"I think communicating with the Nest and working with the octopuses is incredibly important, but I think I'm biased because of my friendship with Charlie. Why do you say it bought us more time?"

Peter said, "Sam, I remember you telling Charlie that having them put the probiotic on white coral was a temporary remedy, that white coral would continue to happen until the ocean temperature dropped. Didn't you believe what you told him?"

"I guess so. But are we there? Mom says the water temperature is still dangerously high."

"It is, but it's not as high as it was last year. And it's not going to get any higher. We now have incredibly effective partners, and the partnership keeps growing. Here, in Cuba, and in Australia, the octopuses are having a significant impact on maintaining coral health."

I said, "Yeah. I wish Dad got to know Charlie."

Mom smiled and looked at Peter, then back to me. "Dad would have been amazed and thrilled if he saw your work communicating with the Nest. But more than that, I wish Dad lived long enough to see you and Jerry grow up. To see you become strong, well-educated people who will make the world better. To see you find wonderful partners. To see the world mend."

Alana said, "I look at you and remember the plucky fourteen-year-old who marched into my lab. You've grown up."

"I guess I have. I remember how angry I was that you kept an octopus in a tank."

"Well, you proved me wrong. You proved us all wrong," Alana said.

I sighed. "God, that seems so long ago. I hardly remember the person I was back then. I think I was angry at everyone."

Jerry said, "I think about all we've been through, all the world has been through, and I get why you were angry. It's been a strange journey, and it isn't over. We still have work to do."

"Well, work can wait," Amanda said. "Let's eat."

About the Author

I've been a jack of all trades of science all my life. Growing up in sputnik era, I played with chemistry sets, built rockets and explored nature. As a young adult,I worked in the field and laboratories for NOAA, NIH, and University of Florida. But I taught science for 36 years. When I retired in 2020, I turned to writing, a passion now that I no longer need a job.

When I'm not writing, my husband and I walk along Tampa Bay, ride our bikes, camp in state parks, visit our adult children and play with our attention-demanding cats.

Life is good.

Also by Ann McNicol

Charlies Story is a series of novels set in the near future, dealing with climate change, genetic engineering and environmental crises.

Charlies Story

Fourteen-year-old Samantha spends her days exploring the shallow reef behind her island home. With her world locked in a battle against rising seas, scientists deploy genetically modified corals to rebuild reefs and protect the coastline. No one expects the reefs to be a hotbed of evolution, but they are.

When an octopus flows off a rock in her lagoon, Samantha is startled. When he purposefully arranges pieces of coral on the sand, trying to communicate, she is shocked. How she responds may determine the fate of life on Earth.

The Nest

The year is 2044. Massive storms and rising sea levels have threatened the continued survival of humanity. A new race of octopuses has gained dominance in the bio-engineered coral reefs. The friendship between fourteen-year-old Samantha and Charlie has deepened as they nurture the extended reef system. When poachers capture Charlie, Samantha must fight to save her friend and maintain their fragile alliance.

Tentacles

The year is 2049. Climate change threatens the extensive reef system, endangering the emerging species of intelligent octopus known as The Nest. Terrifying storms wreak havoc and decimate coastal cities. Samantha and her team work to help the octopuses survive in the face of devastating damage to the reef from a hurricane.

Can the inter-species alliance survive when the octopuses discover humanity's role in climate change and environmental damage? Will the massive campaign to reverse climate change be enough for humanity's survival?

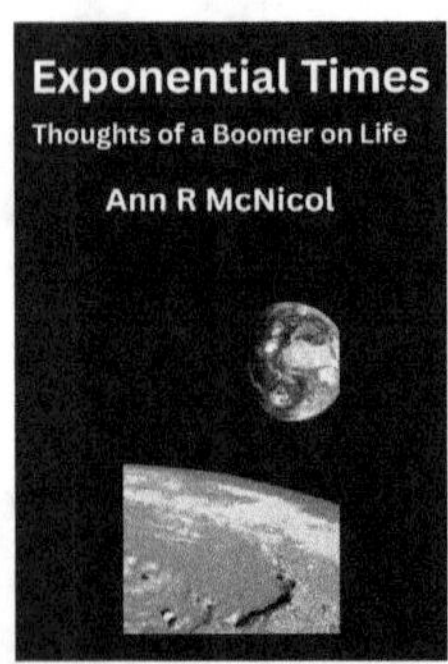

Exponential Times- Thoughts of a Boomer on Life

Getting old is not for the faint at heart but gives perspective. These are just the thoughts and musings of someone who, as a child, watched the first man walk on the moon when television had three channels. Thoughts of a boomer who remembers the world before the internet, before cell phones, and before Amazon.